BATTLE RUNES
Writings on War

BATTLE RUNES
Writings on War

Edited By

GREGORY F. TAGUE

Editions Bibliotekos, Inc.

E♦B

New York

Editions Bibliotekos
Finding the Uncommon Reader

Fredericka A. Jacks, Publisher

Proofreader: Meagan Meehan

Copyright © 2011 by Editions Bibliotekos, Inc.

All Rights Reserved

No part of this book can be copied or distributed in any form or manner whatsoever without permission from the publisher:

publisher@ebibliotekos.com
www.ebibliotekos.com

Printed & Bound in the United States

Set in Garamond

ISBN: 978-0982481943

Editions Bibliotekos, Inc.
E♦B
New York

". . . no man can tell what in that combat attends us, but he that hath been in the battle himself."

- John Bunyan

CONTENTS

Preface,
Fredericka A. Jacks — xi

Foreword,
Wendy Galgan — xiii

Jenny D. Williams,
Go — 1

Hunter Liguore,
Pieces — 3

John Guzlowski,
The German — 9

Mitch Levenberg,
The Marketplace of Lost Dreams — 25

Marko Vešović,
Signature; A Deathless Moment; This Shooting;
Daybreak; I, Too, Like Prince Andrey — 29

Lisa M. Sita,
Triptych (1941-1943) — 37

C.R. Resetarits,
At Sea — 43

John Gifford,
Chance of Rain — 47

Thom Brucie,
A Deepening Heart — 51

Norah Piehl,
Going Somewhere, or Coming Back? 67

Margaret Kingsbury,
The Consequent Phrase of a Melody 75

Lisa L. Siedlarz,
I Dream My Brother Plays Baseball; Insurgent Injured in
Rollover; Who is She?; Commendations; Trauma;
ATF Love; Camels; Don't Paint in Camels;
Mission Accomplished 85

Dawn Sandahl,
The Death of a Phoenix 95

Patty Somlo,
Neither Sweet nor Sour 105

Thom Brucie,
The Tiger Cage 113

Geoffrey A. Landis,
'Abd al Muqeet 129

Muhammad Ashfaq,
The Bombshell 131

Mira Martin-Parker,
Cucumbers 137

Alamgir Hashmi,
Slain Workers Undaunted; Rescue; Camp Office;
Composition in Early Winter 143

Nahid Rachlin,
Gazing at the Stars   149

Nancy Riecken,
Grief Echoes   157

Rebecca Newth,
The Ice Storm   161

Notes on Contributors &
Publication Acknowledgments   166

PREFACE
Fredericka A. Jacks

Battle Runes opens in a child's voice and ends with a child's concern; the book begins in horror and terror and ends with care and hope; the collection starts in darkness and ends in color. The stories and poems – while focused on war – include private and public spaces, often addressing family relationships, such as those between husbands and wives, brothers and sisters, or parents and children. While there is blood in these pages, the emphasis is on the complex psychological dimensions of war. The individual stories cohere around problems of humanity during war, questions about what is humane and what is inhuman.

Wars touched on in this book (from various perspectives) include: the American Civil War, World War I, World War II, the Vietnam War, the African Wars (South Sudan, C.A.R., Congo, Uganda), the Balkan Wars, the Iran-Iraq War, and the Wars in Iraq and Afghanistan. In each and every case the emphasis is on the individual human element, the physical, mental, and spiritual devastation to people who fall victim to social or political forces often beyond their control.

Our editorial approach, considering that this is an anthology of creative writings, has been light-handed: we permit each writer to speak in his or her own voice, with its own distinctive rhythm, syntax, and idiom. We are delighted to present this multi-vocal volume and trust that not only will you find each contribution compelling to read but also will discover how the book (later) is worth pondering in its cumulative emotional and intellectual effect.

FOREWORD

Wendy Galgan

Nations at war – in a world seemingly always at war in one place or another – can lose sight of the cost of battle. A people at war find their perceptions obscured, blurred, obstructed; their focus is too narrow, or too wide. Those caught up in the rush of warfare run the risk of losing their vision, their ability not only to see but also to recognize the terrible cost paid by warrior and civilian alike, by ordinary people facing unbearable losses and witnessing unthinkable tragedies.

The collection you now hold is a remedy to this "war blindness." These authors possess the remarkable ability to allow the reader to see what they see, to take an unsentimental and painfully clear look at what war – fighting it, witnessing it, surviving it – does to human beings. We experience war and its aftermath through the eyes of victor and vanquished, infantry and insurgent, parent and child. We are shown how a shell-shocked vet's "haunted eyes, seeing the lake, were seeing things none of the rest of us could, or would want to, see" ("Going Somewhere, or Coming Back?"). How a young German soldier could look at brutally assaulted women and feel that he "had seen it before and would see it again" because this is the nature of warfare ("The German"). How when "time stands still when the bombs drop and the shells strike," perhaps it does so because "time, unlike you and me, has nothing to lose" and can stand and watch (witness, *see*) what is happening in the combat zone, which could just as well be in an "open field or the crowded marketplace or the quiet sanctuary of someone's home" ("Grief Echoes").

This is a wonderfully varied and extremely powerful collection. We are shown war (and what comes after) in Iran, Africa, Italy and on the Russian front. We see an American medic struggling to save the wounded, the effect of World War I upon a survivor, and shells falling on Sarajevo as a father tries to get his daughter to safety. We are there, witnesses to each battle, observing not from the safety of the sidelines but from the very middle of the action. We watch as soldiers return home to struggle with both the physical and emotional aftereffects of warfare. And we experience the fear of civilians watching their world crumble beneath the machines of war.

These writers are witnesses to the truth of warfare and reveal that truth within these pages. Read on, and see for yourself.

Go

Jenny D. Williams

They came at night, dogs barking and mother said Go. She pushed me from the hut and I ran, I ran fast and faster, away from the village with the other children, naked like me and we fell in the river and it didn't matter. I heard screaming guns dogs barking and then, quiet. We hid in bushes, too small, shivering. Stars were big and blinking and boys don't cry but I did.

They came with knives and we didn't move and they found us anyway. Machete swinging I saw the boy they hit, little like me but then he was dead. Don't try to run away they said and we didn't move. We had white eyes and they had guns. They took the girls, the girls went one way and I don't know where they went.

They made us walk, blisters feet and hungry cold. We grabbed a rope and crossed a river, one boy went under and we didn't see him anymore. Morning came and we lay down. Simon was there, my friend, scared like me with a red shirt and he whispered, Don't ask me about your mother, I won't tell you what I saw.

They got us up and we kept walking, walked long into days and death, bodies in the way with birds hopping pecking, I closed my eyes. Then there was a village, food and water and other little girls and boys.

At the camp a big man came his name was Uncle. Uncle said we should be happy now, we would be men and fight for our land Acholi.

They gave us guns and something up our noses, the girls they stayed inside the huts. We learned the rules and how to load a bullet. Sometimes we heard planes and we would run and hide, dirt came apart and trees and people.

One day I forgot my mother's name and Simon wasn't there and Uncle said it was time.

We went at night, red eyes everyone and full of powder. Crouched and waited at the edge and dark was all around, everything quiet. Then I heard a rustling and Uncle sneaking forward, dogs barking and Uncle said Go. And we ran and ran and don't ask me about what happened then, I won't tell you what I did.

He that will not have peace, God gives him war.

- An old saying

Pieces

Hunter Liguore

I'm picking up pieces: a piece of black fabric in the shape of a square, frayed at the ends and still warm; a chunk of rubber, also black, from the sole of a shoe, which smells like oil; a tuft of dark, black hair, singed on the ends and bent into a curl; a child's finger, no bigger than a cigarette filter, stiff, yet pliable, like a worm to bait a fishing hook; a piece of skin, bloody on one side, rough on the other, resembling a fleck of paint. I collect the pieces – the remains of the boy – into a small, plastic bag. I work fast. I must get the package to the boy's father before he takes him away. Sometimes there's no hurry. Sometimes no one is left alive to collect the injured. Sometimes they die before I can gather everything. The boy still breathes, and so I must hurry.

Behind me, my neighbors run in different directions, like ants that scramble when their mound is stepped upon. People run for shelter, for safety, to divert bullets, another missile, or because they don't know what else to do.

The boy's father lifts his son through a broken car window, close to where I work. The car is deformed; its metal framework melted and shapeless. Flames burn from the backseat. The boy's hand is smeared with purple blood and his index finger is arched in a pointing position. Perhaps he had been pointing at something pretty, something amusing, something only a child could see, but had been cut down before he could share it. The boy's body looks like a pile of rags in the arms of his desperate father. His arm swings as his father runs against the grain of people, and places him on the debris-laden ground.

The father appears calm as he rubs his boy's chest, but his eyes shift around. He's thinking. He is dissolving inside. I imagine he will have thoughts similar to ones that I've had on previous occasions.

What should I do with him? Where will I take him for help? Will I make it in time or will he die in my arms, my only son? Will another bomb explode? Will I get caught in the crossfire? Where's my wife? Does she know to go home? Is she alive? Is she far from here? Does she know she will have to keep the others safe, while I'm tending to our son?

The boy's father wraps the child's dismembered hand with a discarded scarf he finds from the street. The cloth seeps with blood upon contact. The blood won't stop. He searches for something bigger to tie off the wound, but he knows there's internal damage, because of the way the boy's body twists unnaturally. He starts to cry, feeling helpless.

I bring the bag to the father. He takes it from me with little thought. We don't speak to one another. He knows I am there to help. Together, we lift the boy and carry him away.

Gunfire rattles behind the next building, causing more of my people to scurry like hunted game. The women scream through their tears, as their children fall under the rain of bullets. How many times have these mothers warned their children about days like this? Didn't they ingrain in them how to avoid the bullets? Run low, toward the side of the building, hide, run, get away!

The father and I hide behind a building. We see soldiers spreading out into the square. Their green uniforms make them look like tall bushes attacking us. Their M-16's scatter more bullets, more bodies fall. No one is spared, the young, the old, perhaps the lucky.

"Is he still alive?" I ask.

The boy's father nods. I can see the boy's breathing grow heavy, impaired. I've seen this before.

"He was always a good boy. He never..." the man covers his face with his hand. The wet tears clear away the dust from his skin. He never finishes his sentence, nor needs to. I know he wants to say his boy never caused him anger, and never wanted more than he could provide. My boy was just like his. He was about the same age when he was killed in a similar attack six months ago.

The man scoops his boy up in his arms and disappears down the street. The bag I collected for him is gripped in his hand. He doesn't need to thank me. He will appreciate my efforts at a later time. I run in the opposite direction towards home. The gunfire still rages. A second missile explodes toward my left, like an ocean wave, for there is a brief silence before it hits, and then an unfathomable crash, that covers everything in its path.

I run in the direction of the attack, passing through the crowd with resistance. Faces I've known my whole life go by with terror. Their eyes look alien, unfeeling and scared. The missile destroyed a market this time. Arms and legs protrude from the rubble when I arrive. Men gather. Our eyes glance at one another, each hoping the other will move first, as if one of us already has a plan to lead us all to pull the bodies out. I move first, indicating I have the most experience. I yell for someone to help me lift the cement block from the top of the pile. Four hands are not enough. Two others join in, and we're able to slide the block off the top of the mound.

"They may still be alive!" I shout. This gives the others

hope, as they dig with their bare hands through rock, dirt, steel, and blood.

This was how I found my mother. First I found a torn fragment of her scarf covered in the dirt, a piece I keep tied around my wrist in remembrance. After I recovered the rest of the scarf, I found her arm. Upon pulling, the arm came free of her body. I dug quicker, harder, like a monster without emotion, not noticing that I was scraping the skin clean from my fingers. Her eyes were open, staring toward the blue sky, which never seems to change or notice what happens down here. Her body lay contorted in different directions like street signs perched at the corner of an intersection. I tore her body from the tomb, though it was not in my physical strength to do so. The body is as strong as the mind allows.

When the first cadaver is pulled free from the shopping center pit, we are encouraged to go further to find more, but then a child's voice behind us breaks our concentration. We divert our energy to the definite living. Beneath the rubble, a boy has found a breathing space; he calls for his brother. Someone goes for him. The rest of us dig. Sweat pours down my face as I work with the others to lift the stone and rubble, to free the boy. We all know with one wrong move, we could bury him.

The boy's brother comes. Upon seeing his younger brother buried, the brother screams for Allah to do something, anything to keep him alive. His hands dig and lash at the gravel to reach him. "You're not going to die! Do you hear me?" the brother says with strength. I used to pray to Allah, until I realized that he could not hear my prayers over the bombing and gunfire.

Gunfire cuts over our heads. We drop to our bellies.

"Quickly!" someone says. "We must go!" shouts another man. Several escape over the mound.

"We can come back," I say to the brother. "He's safe where he is."

The soldiers spot us. Though we lie grotesquely upon the ruins of the building, and the remains of life, with little left for them to take, but our lives, they come. A bullet grazes my head as I pull the brother's arm to leave. My head spins; my ears ring. More gunfire. The brother's chest spurts blood when three bullets pass through his body. I roll to the other side of the debris pile, watching, as the brother's brains spill out onto the cement stone like vomit, as the deadening bullet pierces his skull. I hear the boy screaming below. He is terrorized, no longer a boy, but a caged lion, crazed with fear.

Children take to the rooftop of a building on the other side of the street and throw rocks down upon the soldiers, who return fire willingly. The boys are quick to hide, and their efforts give me enough time to get away.

Blood runs down my cheek. I keep wiping it, but it still flows. I am dizzy, but determined. After the soldiers leave, I return to the mound. New faces arrive to help clean the debris and dig for loved ones. I notice the boy doesn't call out anymore. I remove a plastic bag from my pocket. I keep a few with me at all times. I can never tell when I might need one.

When my boy was killed in an attack, a month before my mother, his body lay in pieces on the gravel road. As his father I should've been able to pick him up and put him back together. I sat beside my dead son for what felt like an entire season, until someone stirred me, a man, who handed me a plastic bag with my son's remains. Every piece is sacred, he said. He did this for me so I didn't have to; it was the most loving act anyone has ever done for me. My son was my first loss, then my mother was taken, then my wife and three girls. My whole family has been slain during one attack or another. I have no one left, but my neighbors. They are what's important now.

I don't know if anyone would come for the two brothers. Sometimes they do. Sometimes they're never claimed. I didn't know if the boy was still alive, or if he would live. I half knew he was already dead – his silence confirming what I knew in my heart – but the hopeful side of me did not want to admit the truth. I bagged the soft, slick brain. Beside the body was a crushed flower. Its color purple stood out from the disaster. I put this into the bag too. I laid it on the brother's chest and forced his eyes closed. I carried him to the end of the row of bodies already collecting in the street. I looked at the faces for anyone I might know, but I knew them all in one way or another.

I searched for the first boy and his father, but he was not there. Perhaps he lived, or maybe I half knew he was already dead. He probably died in his father's arms, just like mine did. The hopeful side of me wasn't ready to admit anything with certainty. A missile soared overhead, crashing in the plaza several blocks away. I ran against the grain to get there, a body in pieces waiting. I took out another plastic bag and began picking up pieces.

The German

John Guzlowski

With the barrel of his rifle, he slowly pushed the door open, but he didn't enter. The log hut's single room was like all of the rooms he'd seen since crossing the border into Russia. There was a mud floor, a wooden table, and two rough-cut chairs. In the corner next to the stove stood an empty wooden pen where they had kept some kind of small animal, perhaps a pig or calf. On the table, a lamp burned unsteadily, flickered like the fuel had been mixed with water. In the shadows he saw an old woman asleep in a bed. The bed smelled of wet and sour rags. He could smell it from a dozen feet away.

He wondered how people could live like this, in small rooms with dirt and animals, and so little light that a man had to spend his life squinting at things, struggling to see clearly. But outside it was already dark, and the snow was falling harder, so he entered.

Raising his rifle, he walked over to the old woman lying in the bed. Her eyes and mouth were open, a babushka hid her hair but he knew it must be thin and gray. Her skin was gray too, a yellow gray. This woman was old the way the earth was old in the late fall, spent with spring and summer work, tired of doing everything that needed to be done each day.

The soldier stood above her next to the bed and felt the weight of his rifle in his hands. Even after four years of carrying it, it was still heavy. He wanted to put it down, and he wanted many other things too. He wanted warmth first and then safety. Yes, safety would be good, and a wife and food and a God who would take pity on him and send His only Beloved Son to do the killing the man felt he couldn't do anymore. But he knew too that wishing and praying were useless. He'd seen the ashes of too many churches and synagogues. He'd settle for food.

He poked the old woman's shoulder with the barrel of his Mauser.

At first she didn't move at all, and he thought she must be ill or weak from hunger, but then she moved a little. She drew in a ragged breath and then another. Her breathing was grim and harsh. There was no sweetness to it. She drew the breath deep into her lungs slowly like she was filling a glass past overflowing. He poked her again, and she opened her eyes slowly and looked at him without moving her head.

There was cold and silence in the room, but he didn't sense any fear. In peddler's Russian he said, "Grandmother, I'm hungry."

She didn't say anything. He felt her staring at him. She probably knew by his accent and gray uniform that he was a German. Then, she nodded with her eyes and began to rise. Her right hand gripped the edge of the bed, and her body tensed for the work of lifting itself. Like her breathing, the rising was grim and painful. Old people carry burdens that would break a young man's faith and hope.

The German sat down on one of the clumsy wooden chairs and looked at the old woman. Maybe once she was young and had some life in her veins, but now she was like a dead creature, like something left in a barn for too long, a cow whose fat and muscle had thinned in a dry season when the grass was burnt and gone by the first of July.

He watched her as she walked slowly to the door and

closed it. Then she moved over to a small porcelain stove. It's pretty, he thought – a creamy white with large green flowers on the oven door. He wondered how it got here to this shack in the middle of this flat, dead country. There was nothing else in the room that spoke of wealth like this stove did. He felt there must be a story to it, but he didn't want to ask. A story would just slow her down, and he was hungry.

He slapped the palm of his hand on the table once and shouted in German that he wanted food and he wanted it quickly, *"Mach schnell, frau, essen, essen!"* The sharp noise and the shouting did not startle her. The old woman continued to move slowly, lighting a match to the crumpled newspaper in the stove, closing the door, dragging a large wooden box across the floor with both hands so it would be near the stove.

Then, she started taking metal cans out of the box. They were army issue. Some had big German lettering, some had Russian. One of the large cans had script that was neither German Gothic nor Russian Cyrillic. He couldn't make it out in the shadows.

Maybe it was Japanese. The letters looked like pagodas and huts and trees. He wondered how she came by these cans, and imagined some soldier from the war between Russia and Japan, the old one, the one fought in the high desert country of Mongolia and Korea, passing through here forty or fifty years ago and trading the cans for a look at her breasts or a poke at her cunt. Maybe fifty years ago she was something to look at, still a girl then, a blonde, moving like a slow cool breeze on a hot day. Now she moved like a spent mule on a cold day, broken and shivering.

He knew that pounding his palm on the table wouldn't get her moving any faster. This woman moved as she moved. She was bone and hanging skin and breathing that came from the center of the earth, all harsh and ragged whispers.

He took his steel helmet off and unwound the rags that kept his ears warm. Then, he ran his hand through his hair. It was matted and greasy, and he felt lice and fleas there, spending the winter like they were millionaires on some sun bleached Riviera beach. He scratched his head with both hands lightly so as not to draw blood, and he tried to remember the last time he bathed. It was a month ago probably. Some place farther east, maybe near Kursk, when his squad had to guard a ford that the Mark IV's were going to use to cross over a stream so they could get out of the way of the Russians. He and the others waited for two days for those tanks. The hollow boom of artillery firing in the distance disrupted their days, and in the nights they could see flashes too, purple and yellow against the clouds, filling the sky like bruises. The waiting men took turns bathing in the water upstream from the ford, first the boys in the squad and then the old men. The boys splashed and laughed and tried to dunk each other; the old men stood in silence in the water washing their faces and hands. And always while some bathed, others watched and listened for the partisans. A place like that was full of them, and a small squad alone at a stream was like hot milk sweetened with honey to the Russians.

He looked at the old woman again. She had opened a can with a key and was heating some kind of meat in thick, dark brown gravy. He wondered if she knew any partisans. Maybe her son was with them, or her daughter, or her husband. The German knew she had probably seen her fill of killing. She must be sixty or seventy. How many dead had she seen in her life? Ten? Fifty? A hundred? And who were they? Children?

Husbands? Parents? Grandparents? Neighbors? Too many to remember all of their names, he thought. If you lived long enough, the dead you knew outnumbered the living, and they were closer to you.

And now this war. Three years of armies moving across her land. If she looked out her door any summer morning, she would see the soldiers or their dust. Hear them too if the wind was coming from the right direction. Smell them too. It would be better in the winter perhaps. Like now. With a heavy wet snow falling, you couldn't hear or smell anything more than ten meters away. Couldn't see it either, not even five meters away. Your home would be safe, hidden from the soldiers, unless they fell upon it by accident as they were fleeing or rushing forward.

He raised his head and said, "I bet I startled you, little mother. Coming in like I did with you lying there, maybe even sleeping. I bet it made your heart jerk. I bet you felt like a young girl again, a yellow-haired maiden with flowers in her hands waiting for her first kiss behind the church."

The woman stopped stirring the meat in the shallow, black pan, and looked at him. She was bent like a willow, and the skin on her face and hands was hard and cracked with the cold, despite the fat she had rubbed into it. The hand with the wooden spoon was almost shut completely with arthritis. Her fingers thin and crippled like tree limbs, her knuckles fat and red. Her eyes didn't say much, just that she had been here before, fed other men, knew how to give them what they wanted so they would leave her alone.

She turned back to her stirring, and the German looked away from her. There was a window in this hut, and where the newspaper she had pressed against the window had pealed back, he could see the snow falling, coming down harder. He knew that by the time night came he wouldn't be able to leave this hut, if he was still here. But where could he go? There were no towns nearby, only armies fumbling in the cold and the dark, pressing here and there, and hoping that the morning would show that their blind movements had brought them some small advantage.

Suddenly, he wanted to talk. For days he'd been alone, ever since his squad had entered that ravine and they were ambushed by the partisans hiding in a stand of birch trees.

His comrades died there, slowly at first, then quicker and quicker. The bullets ricocheting off the rocks and boulders with a terrible zwingging noise, trees exploding into splinters, splinters burning quickly and spreading their fire to the twigs and underbrush. There was nowhere to hide from that noise and the fire and the splintering wood that would kill a man slower than a bullet but as surely. First one of the sergeants fell, and then another. Peter fell with a wrist-thick piece of oak embedded in his throat like a wooden lightning bolt. He had been with the German since they crossed the border into Poland three years ago. Then the Hungarian boy Jurek dropped, then it was happening so fast that the German could not say, this one fell next and then that one fell. All he knew was that he had to run, get away from the ravine and the Russians. He crawled back up the hill, the way his squad had come down. And while he crawled, bullets picked at him, hit at him, moved him this way and then that, but still he kept climbing up the ravine. He felt like an old man crawling up a sand dune under a load of bricks that was getting heavier and heavier with each bullet that ripped at his clothes and cut at his skin. But he didn't stop till he crested the hill and left behind the ravine with his dead comrades.

He had left dead men behind before and he knew that it would hurt him only for a little while. The next day, Peter and Jurek and the others would just be the dead.

The soldier stared at the old woman again. He wanted her to say something; he needed to hear a voice. "Mother," he asked in Russian, "do you live here alone?"

She didn't say anything; she kept stirring the canned meat with her crooked fingers. Her back was too him, but he knew she had heard him because she had stopped stirring for a second when he first asked the question.

He tried again. "Mother, do you live alone in this hut?"

She turned her head and looked at him. "I live here with my husband; he's out looking for the pig. She got away yesterday when the soldiers came."

"A pig? I'm surprised there's anything left here. This war's not easy on pigs."

She moved toward him, placed a plate on the table. She didn't offer him a knife or fork, but he didn't expect her to. He had the ones the army gave him, his first day as a soldier. They were bright as the chrome on a new Mercedes roadster then.

"Rest while I eat," he said, and gestured for her to sit across from him on the other chair.

She moved instead to the bed and sat down on the comforter. It was a pale red color and thin, almost flat. The goose feathers in it were old; they must have lost their fullness, their fatness, a generation ago. She put her hands in her lap and looked at him without speaking.

"Why are you so quiet?" he said. "I bet when your old man is around you're a regular hen, pecking and clucking at him.

Tell me something, anything. Tell me what's it been like here this fall?"

She shrugged and sat in silence, her eyes on his eyes. Then she started speaking slowly. She told him that the fall had been hard so far. Early in October, there was rain and mud, and then the cold started and the mud froze. She liked it when the mud froze. She didn't like the smell of the mud when it was wet – it was like manure, like living in a toilet. It was better when the muck froze. She could walk outside and not worry about the mud sucking her boots off. Her husband lost a rubber boot once right outside the door. The mud was like a demon, it just sucked the boot right off his foot, like a giant mouth. Her husband never found the boot. Not even in the spring.

The German thought about what she said, the mud like a giant mouth. Here in Russia he had seen mud like that, seen men disappear into the mud and never appear again. He'd felt it pulling him under more than once too. He could picture in his mind this mud like a mouth – and it was almost like a short movie, one that you would expect a dancing and singing mouse in gloves and a tuxedo to appear in, scolding the old woman's husband for stepping on the mud. The German thought about this mud like a giant's mouth and the dancing mouse and started laughing, deep laughs, loud and long. He imagined the mouse singing something in Italian, maybe a happy song of love and hope from some opera. It was a funny thought, and after a while he stopped laughing, and then he picked up the brown-gray meat with his fork. He looked at it for a second and bit off a piece.

Chewing, he watched the woman stare at him. She'd stopped talking. He knew his laughter must have made her nervous. He was a German sitting in her hut with a rifle leaning against her table, and he was laughing. She must fear what would come next. He watched her pull something out of her pocket. It looked like a leather shoestring. Her arthritic, twisted fingers started worrying it, knotting it and unknotting it.

The meat in his mouth was hard, stringy with gristle. He knew it was horsemeat but he was hungry, and just having something in his mouth to chew made him happy. He already felt the meat's warmth in his stomach, and he remembered when he was a boy eating bread with butter after a long day of fasting and waiting for the communion host. The old nuns used to say that God wanted us to wait because patience brought us closer to him.

He pointed at the old woman with his knife and hoped she saw the smile through his beard. "Go on," he said, "tell me some more."

She began again. This time she told him about how the pig was lost. Yesterday morning as the snow and the wind were slowing, she told him, there was a loud knock at the door and before she and her husband could get out of bed, two soldiers came in, Russians, her own people.

The old woman said to the German, "One of them was short like a boy, but he wasn't a boy. He had a beard and an angry voice."

He said, "We're taking your pig," and he moved to the wooden pen against the wall. Her husband got out of bed quickly then and stepped in front of the soldier.

"Please, sirs, don't take our pig," he said. "It's all we have to get us through this winter. The harvest was nothing, as you know, sirs, and much of what we grew was taken for our boys in the army."

She told the German how the short, angry soldier pushed her husband aside and loosened a rope he had in his hands. He and the other soldier entered the pen and tied a harness across the pig's neck and chest. While the pig squealed and kept trying to push back from the soldiers, the woman and her husband pleaded, even though they knew pleading was worthless. Soldiers take what they want.

When the soldiers dragged the pig out of the hut, she and her husband followed into the cold and snow. They knew that nothing would bring the pig back, but they could not let it go.

She pleaded with the angry soldier, "Please give us some piece of writing that will say you soldiers took our pig. We could show it to our village headman, and he would get us something in exchange, maybe some rubles or some flour."

Pulling the pig, the short soldier said, "Mother, I'd give you a receipt if I could, but I can't write and my comrade here, he's a fool and he can't write either." He laughed as he said this and shoved the pig along with his boot.

Then, there was an explosion in the falling snow. The short soldier died where he stood. A shell exploded his head and scattered red and purple pieces across the front of the wooden hut and the snow on the ground around him. The other soldier didn't even have time to unshoulder his rifle. There was another explosion in the falling snow, and he dropped to his knees, a spreading red stain growing darker and bolder on his gray tunic. He was dead before his face touched the dirty snow. The startled pig jerked the rope loose from the headless soldier's hands, scurried across the frozen furrows, and was immediately lost in the snow.

"That's when my husband took off," she said. "My

husband took off after the pig. He stumbled in the snow and raised himself and stumbled again. He's an old man, and his legs aren't much. He disappeared into the snow on his knees."

The German didn't wait for the story to end. He couldn't stop laughing. He dropped the fork and wiped away the tears with his hand. Really, he thought, this story is better than the Laurel and Hardy films they show in Magdeburg. The old woman had the gypsy's gift for storytelling, and he thought again about her husband falling and crawling after the pig.

"Mother," the soldier said, "pardon my laughing. You must be thinking, just like a German to be laughing at another's misfortune, but I haven't laughed this way since we retreated across the River Desna. If I had a *kopec*, I'd give it to you."

She frowned and slowly shook her head from side to side in disapproval.

When he stopped laughing, he asked for another piece of meat and chewed it after she gave it to him. He wasn't used to food and the heat in the room, slight as it was. They made him drowsy. Soon he would want to sleep, but he was afraid of that. This woman was Russian, and even though she might blame the Russian soldiers for the loss of her pig and her husband, the German knew he couldn't trust her not to kill him while he slept. He'd heard plenty of stories about Germans dying with their throats cut in some Russian peasant's shack. And he'd seen too many dead German soldiers sitting at wooden tables with their tunics unbuttoned and their boots off. Maybe if he tied her up he'd be safe – safe from her at least.

He pushed the empty plate away and asked her for some rope, just enough to hobble a horse.

She looked at him and started talking softly, "Why do you

want a rope? Are you going to strangle me, or tie me up and take me somewhere? What if my husband comes back with the pig and finds me gone? What will he say? He's like me, old and weak. We don't make war on soldiers, or anyone. We couldn't even stop the soldiers from taking the pig. Or the cow before that. Or the grain even before that."

"Don't worry," he said. "I won't take you away. Why would I want to drag an old witch like you anywhere? And where would we go? Back to Berlin? You'd be a prize catch. Better than a Soviet general. Better than your holy Stalin. I just want to tie you up so that I can sleep peacefully without you cutting my throat with your butcher knife."

"I'm sure, but what if your husband comes back and finds me here asleep, maybe he'll think I'm trying some funny business with you, and he'll try to shoot me. Or maybe the two of you will try to kill me."

"You don't have to worry. He's an old man with lungs that are thin like paper. And a bad back, too. He won't try to do anything to hurt you."

"Shut up. This isn't a debate. I'm going to tie you up."

In the shadows at the other end of the room, he saw a stretch of rope hanging from the pig pen, and took it and cut it into two lengths. Then he ordered her to sit in the other chair. With one length he tied her hands up, with the other he tied her feet. Then, he picked her up and carried her to the bed. He put her near the edge and covered her with part of the red comforter.

She said nothing and lay with her face pressed to the mattress.

He looked at her and wondered what she was thinking. She was probably afraid, he imagined. An old woman, brittle bones, not much strength in her hands and legs, tied up by a German soldier – she must be thinking he was going to torture her, or rape her. She was surely afraid. And she was right to be. Some would take a poke at her – no matter that she was 60 or 70. A soldier, German, Russian, English, Hungarian, American, Italian, whatever, out here in this frozen muck, wandering around like a gypsy without home or family, would take her and spread her and be happy for the moment's comfort no matter how much she fought, no matter how much she pleaded.

The German drifted away for a second and saw again the bodies of the dead women he came across last week. They were scattered like dominoes out next to a barn, a dozen of them, some young as school girls, some like this woman, old and broken, and all their skirts were lifted up, bloody and twisted hard with mud. These women, he knew, must have been raped until they could not scream. He had seen this kind of thing before. The women were raped even when they were dead, just so one last soldier could pause for a moment in the middle of this war and forget that he himself was a dead man. The German had seen it before and would see it again. The road from here back to Berlin was long.

He shook his head and thought, here we are, yes, here we are, the world in all its glory and beauty.

He looked again at the old woman, and she was staring up at him. There was nothing in her eyes, no worry or fear. She just looked tired, like she wanted all of this stupidity, the war and the lost pig and the husband who disappeared into the falling snow, to end.

He turned away from her and stepped to the table and the lamp. He turned the knob and the weak flame flickered even more, and then it died. The darkness in the room was tinged with a purple light, a darkness mixed with light reflected from the snow still falling outside. He remembered that this was how the nights looked when he was a young boy in Magdeburg playing outside in the street late in the evening after a heavy snow fall, the mysterious purple light that came from nowhere and came from everywhere. There was beauty in it, and magic too. It felt like the whole world was waiting on his pleasure, like God Himself was staring down from heaven, His elbows spread across a giant windowsill, and He was smiling at him playing in the snow, rolling snow boulders in the night, and maybe it was God's smile that showered a purple light across the dark, snow-crusted world.

The German shook himself back to the moment. He was tired and thinking too much. Soon he'd be weeping and falling on his knees. He knew he needed sleep.

He made his way to the bed, and climbed over the old lady. She said nothing, not a groan even when his weight pressed down on her for a moment. If she had, maybe he would have asked her pardon. Instead, he pulled the comforter over himself and wondered why it was red. Did Stalin give a red comforter to every woman who gave birth to a strong son or a fecund daughter? The German smiled in the dark at the thought of Stalin, the great Soviet Grandfather with smoking pipe and perpetual smile and work camps and prison camps and five-year plans that left poor people staring into empty cups. The German moved closer to the old woman. He hoped for some warmth, but there wasn't much.

He knew it would be a cold night. He heard the wind outside. It was like a broom sweeping ice into the world. The door and the wall and the windows would not keep this blizzard out. In the morning, he knew, there would be snow on the frozen mud floor. He snuggled against the old woman, pulled her closer to him gently, and tried to will himself to sleep, tried to empty his thoughts, but couldn't.

He thought about how some morning he would not rise, would not wake. Some night, the cold would take him before dawn, and some fellows would find his body then, stiff as a plank. They would leave him where they found him, frozen across some path or next to some fence he had leaned against to keep the wind from his stomach and genitals, his soft parts. If he was lucky and the ground was not frozen, the men who found him might drop him in a shallow grave. He'd seen that plenty. A shallow grave with a frozen foot sticking out. It made him laugh sometimes. There's something funny about a foot poking out of the snow. A frozen hand was a different thing. You see that hand and you know someone had gone down hard, probably pleading at the last, begging for his mother, even in death. Yes, a hard death.

"Happy thoughts for a cold night," he said aloud and wondered if the old woman next to him was still awake. She said nothing, and he couldn't hear her breathing.

He wondered what kept her alive. The pig and her husband? Her duty to them? They were gone and wouldn't come back. Maybe the husband would, but certainly not the pig. The way the old woman told that story, the German knew her husband didn't have the strength to both pursue the pig and then bring it home. He was probably out there some place, pressed against a slight rise of earth, frozen and dead.

The German's face felt stiff from the frost on his moustache and beard. He could feel the ice in his feet and his calves as well. It made him wonder if he would be able to walk far tomorrow, or whether he would be able to walk at all. Today, before he found the old woman's hut, he had covered maybe ten kilometers, not enough to make him feel safe.

He leaned further into the old woman. His knees pressed against the back of her legs, his chest against her back. He felt that her old bones, her rags, her thin flesh must still have a little human warmth left in them to share with another. He tried to pull her even closer.

But where was the warmth? It was like Siberia in the hut.

◊ ~♦~ ◊

War to the castles, peace to the cottages.

- An old saying

◊ ~♦~ ◊

The Marketplace of Lost Dreams

Mitch Levenberg

It is May 13, 1945 and my father and his unit have reached the 5th Replacement Depot "a few miles beyond Las Pinas." On the way from Manila he views some of the local color: "Our trip from Manila to our camp was interesting and picturesque. Passed quaint homes; thatched roofs on bamboo huts and quaint primitive shops selling odd fruits and a profusion of oddities. . . they sold minnows and various grasses which the people eat around here."

In the foreground of one of my father's photos is an open area just outside what looks like, in the background, a large marketplace, itself shaded by a long, flat roof that moves beyond the photo, though how far no one can tell. Perhaps it forms a semi-circle or perhaps it ends just a few more feet beyond where the photo can no longer contain it. The photo, the camera, takes in as much of the structure, as much of the activity as possible but can go only so far. The activity, even the structure, resists any attempt to control or contain it, to freeze it in some kind of falsely eternal context.

In the middle of the open courtyard a single American soldier, awkward, gangly, reluctant, slightly bent like a tree against the wind, stands perfectly still, his stillness a perfect contrast to the movement around him. Native Filipinos, dressed mostly in white, move, in the blazing hot whiteness of the sun, in a myriad of directions, their elongated shadows lingering so far behind them they seem like separate entities. Many of the people seem to come from outside the photo or else are on the verge of leaving it, part of their bodies inside, part outside, as if walking in and out of a dream. There appears to be no order or reason to their movement, yet at the same time their movement seems like some human necessity, as if movement, the lack of order and reason is the norm. Indeed, everyone seems reasonable and calm – human purpose and habit, the ingredients of survival, the intensity and urgency reflect the time, that not to move is death, to move is life, survival, purpose. So there is a calmness, a certainty perhaps in the need to always be moving, that to live, to survive is to move.

On the other hand, the soldier seems to be without purpose, without meaning, an alien, out of place, out of time. He stands droopingly, forlornly, purposeless on the very outskirts of this marketplace of lost dreams. And yet, isn't he their savior? Isn't this drooping and lifeless image a part of the great war machine that is their savior? How can this be? What does it all mean? And besides, do they really see him? If anything, he seems merely a ghost of that machine, a spectral, yet necessary ingredient of a nightmare from which these people, one day, one year, hope to awake.

In the background of the photo, inside what appears to be the marketplace itself, there is no movement, no light. Here is only the shadowy suggestion of humanity, small clots of natives, for the moment stilled, stagnant, resigned. This is where life contracts, where it comes face to face, sometimes literally, with the bare bones of survival. Is it food they are buying, the odd assortments of grass, minnows, festering meat? It is hard to tell, but if you look hard enough, you can perhaps see (though by no means is this certain) an old woman's face, as if you were seeing it in a dream, fading in and out, alert and hopeful, pained and deadened, real and not real; just a shadow or an old woman's face, it is hard to tell.

The only thing certain is the photo itself, the hot whiteness of the sun, the stillness of the soldier, and the eternal swirl that surrounds him.

◊ ~◆~ ◊

War destroys many for the benefit of the few.

- Menander

◊ ~◆~ ◊

BATTLE RUNES

◊ ~◆~ ◊

A little group of wise hearts is better than a wilderness of fools.

- John Ruskin

War should be long in preparing in order that you may conquer the more quickly.

- Publilius Syrus

◊ ~◆~ ◊

Signature
(Potpis)

Marko Vešović

All translations by Omer Hadžiselimović

Something has changed between me and people since I became a parent to one of them. – Paul Claudel

I'm running home with my little daughter –
again, shells have surprised us on the street.
Shells have, for centuries, been falling every day,
and every time they surprise us.
I'm hurrying her on with angry words,
transferring my rage from the Serb gunners
to a child awaited ten years.
Let me write my name, she tells me, as we pass
a patch of virgin snow in the park.
Instead of scolding her,
I – God knows why – let her forefinger
break the delicate whiteness,
and then, around the Cyrillic IVANA VEŠOVIĆ
my forefinger describes a circle,
impenetrable

like in fairy-tales.

BATTLE RUNES

A Deathless Moment
(Besmrtan tren)

A sniper is working a street crossing.
Two girls, breathless from running across.
They radiate heat, perfumed, like silk
underwear being ironed. One of them doesn't have a hairdo,
but bristling wheat sprouts on her head. She's fuming,
thundering, and cursing at the snipers: I seem to be watching,
like out of a window,
a glorious storm!
   The other's words are pleasant
like the fluttering of an umbrella, in the morning, at the Budva
                  beach.
She tosses her head from time to time. For our sake!
For she knows: with each toss, her long hair will smell sweetly.
A beauty. But one of those who never fail
to smile at you. Both lavishly and stingily.
Lavishly enough to make you happy. Stingily enough
that it costs them nothing. Their smile
lets you know that for them you are not a thing among things.
They wish perhaps to break the spell put on you
by an icy female look that has turned you into a thing.

The air smelled sweetly of my youth of long ago
when every tree-lined lane led to the end of the world.

When the soul could, even in a desert,

Start singing like a woman reaper.
When life was not yet *worn thin like a proverb*.
They left, chattering, leaving in me the tenderness
that comes over you when you look long at the skies
swarming with snowflakes.
They went. Not two girls,
but two breezes, blowing suddenly
through scorching heat of the siege.

Through the dog days of existence.

This Shooting
(Ova pucnjava)

This shooting has gotten into our blood. Without shooting
(just like without your morning coffee) you can't get your day
                                                            going.
And do you remember how, at the start of the war, after a
                                                    shell
burst a hush would descend,
like the deadly silence when someone
in a bar blabbed something against Tito or the Party?
Shells have now gotten into our bones. When there is a
                                             silence,
you're as taut as a string. You keep thinking: My God, what
                                                    are

they fixing for us now? With that silence they only instill more
fear into our bones. But as soon as a heavy machine gun
                                      makes itself heard,
I loosen up right away, my wife begins making a pie,
the kids start chattering around the house. They are shooting
                                                  again –
everything's all right, then. Yesterday, back home from work,
I asked: was there any shooting while I was gone?
My youngest daughter told me: *You should have seen, Dad,
how nicely two of them whizzed by!*

Daybreak
(Svitanje)

I'm doing sentry duty. At dawn. Nearby is a house.
Actually, a yellowish hovel. Beside it a poplar
Above a well. The poplar is as tall, it somehow
Seems to me, as the well is deep.
Above the house, as above Ithaca, white smoke
is unfolding, like a baby's swaddling-clothes.

In the house a child is crying. Long. For years already.
It seems: The shack would come down if the child fell silent.
All sorts of things come to mind when one is doing sentry
                                                              duty.

MARKO VEŠOVIĆ

All of a sudden, a golden-headed chit of a girl comes out of
                                                    the house,

She's about ten years old, twelve, at the most. Missing a leg.
A gorgeous invalid. A cherub on crutches.
With a ruddy face, as if from the daybreak.
And tears welled up in my eyes. From that ruddiness on her
                                                              face.
From that daybreak on crutches! All kinds of things can
                                            engross your mind
When you are doing sentry duty.

And the child's weeping seems never to stop. As if it had
its own electric motor. The weeping which, it seems,
will not cease, as long as this world exists. As long as there is
a soul alive under these skies. A weeping that will
resound through all eternities.

For time, when you are a sentry, moves slowly like a glacier.
On sentry, your soul sometimes hears galloping Tartar
                                                    messengers
bringing the news that, under these skies,
There's nothing. Not even you. On sentry duty.

There is only smoke. Not the one above Ithaca.
But the one from the sentence, written in Etruscan –
The first that science succeeded to decode:
Man is nothing but smoke.

BATTLE RUNES

I, Too, Like Prince Andrey
(I ja sam ko knez Andreja)

from a green meadow, wounded, was staring at the eternal
                                                          sky.
There was nothing for a million miles around.
Yes, miles, as if the immense void that
roared around me was in fact the open sea.
Stark and boundless. From everything, under the sky,
only a blind starkness remained that roared brutally.

At first, to be sure, Serb frogs could be heard
in Dobrinja's pools. But they soon fell silent.
Oh, wonder of wonders: a chorus of frogs is bidding me
                                                      farewell
to the other world (I thought, if that could be
called thinking. For it was my skin that was thinking).

I, too, like Prince Andrey, before death,
          suddenly felt that there was nothing in the world
but that immeasurable distance
above me, and the still more immeasurable distance,
inside. As if the soul was looking upon itself
from an immensity powerfully healing.
Or as if it were looking on its pain after a million summers.
Pain turned into a white waterfall
          roaring like the spring of the Bosna.

MARKO VEŠOVIĆ

I, too, like Prince Andrey, realized
        that nothing matters more
than those distances that multiplied with lightning speed.
Seventy-seven immensities,
        the soul drinking from each
like from the seventy-seven fountains
        of my home.
The world was, all around, ground to powder,
        and looked like that
ruddy column of dust that surges upward
when a shell smashes into someone's house in Sarajevo.

And I understood that those far distances
can only come to the good.
And you are happy
        because, in those distances,
you are a tiny wisp,
but a wisp containing all those distances.

And I felt those distances
suddenly pouring into me,
        like Krka Falls near Knin,
but a million times bigger. With a million rainbows
created in the watery dust.

And I listened to those distances
        rushing to cleanse me from the inside,
to wash the blood stains in which
the whole world had been dissolved.

~

BATTLE RUNES

◊ ~♦~ ◊

The drums of war, the drums of peace,
Roll through our cities without cease.

- R.L. Stevenson

Far from the din of war, the kindly earth pours forth
an easy sustenance.

- An old saying

◊ ~♦~ ◊

Triptych (1941 – 1943)

Lisa M. Sita

The guns were stationed on the outskirts of Careri, four cannon overlooking the main road and the valley below, facing the sea. They had become a familiar feature to the townspeople, a common fixture, but not one so recognizable that it ceased to disturb them. The presence of the guns, with their piles of ammunition, would never fade into the mundane and predictable. They were there always on the edge of the people's collective consciousness. Meant as protection, they remained a low-lying, constant threat of hulking metal and explosive powder.

The guns, and the soldiers who manned them, were not easily visible to the people as they went about their daily lives. Men and women, perched in the twisted branches of the olive trees on the slopes of the mountains, did not look for them as they hand-picked olives or stood below the trees, striking branches with sticks until the olives tumbled down into the nets spread out on the ground below. At the local press, where each family's portion was separated into stone troughs to be pressed individually, the smooth brown olives crushed whole – delicate skin, savory meat, and pits – under the heavy horse-pulled grinding stones, the people did not cower in anticipation that the guns would go off. The workers at the press carried on calmly, packing the olive paste into woven rounds that were pressed from above until the golden oil, squeezed from the pulp, dripped through the mesh into vats of water below to be strained off and bottled.

The guns could not be seen from the grist mill, where the people arrived bearing bags of wheat slung over the backs of donkeys, and where, between the heavy stone wheels of the mill, the grain was crushed into fine flour by the sweat of the horses that pulled the ropes that kept the mechanism in motion. Nor were the guns detectable in the evenings, when the people had returned from the fields, when the craftsmen and storekeepers had closed their shops, and when women had sat down after clearing the kitchen of the day's labor or ironing the last of the shirts hung out to dry on the balcony.

As neighbors walked up the twilight streets to visit one another, to talk and gossip, to play cards by the light of kerosene lamps, and as the night deepened with the tremolo of mandolins and the soft strumming of guitars drifting out in melodious waves over the darkened roofs and quiet streets, the people always knew that the guns, poised and waiting, lay close on the edge of their town.

And then, within the passing of the year, a steady visitation of planes began to pull the people's attention upward. The planes always came in the darkness, every night, little birds gliding through the soft, black sky. They flew in flocks, passing over the mountains on to the cities of the valleys and coasts below. In their iron throats they carried their death song, a rumbling, mechanical buzz that spread across the sky and reverberated through the air before falling to the earth below.

Every night the people of Careri watched the planes in the distance, knew that in the cities all would be rushing for the air raid shelters to the sound of sirens whipping high-pitched warnings through the streets and *piazze*. On the mountain, from their quiet balconies and darkened windows, the townspeople watched the bombs released from the bellies of the planes like tiny eggs freefalling, black against the night sky. They watched the splintered show of fireworks, points and rods of luminous light spitting up from the ground. Then in an instant, sparks flashing into slow-burning flames, small tufts of orange brilliance.

There was nothing they could do. They shook their heads and frowned, mumbled prayers, made the sign of the cross. They looked at one another piteously, cursed the war, spoke of other things. In the silence of their beds they feared, hoped for peace, evoked the saints, held the hands of those they loved.

One time they heard news that the entrance to a shelter in one of the cities had been hit, and that six hundred people had been killed. There were no shelters in Careri. The town was too high up on the mountain to have any strategic usefulness, and so it was spared the attention of the planes. But the townspeople saw, they witnessed, and they breathed lighter, thankful for their insignificance even while grieving for the people below.

In the mornings the sun would come up, spreading light and warmth across the mountains, into the valleys, and over the coasts out to sea. The sound of vendors calling out their wares as they pulled carts through the winding streets would shake the quiet of Careri. Doors would open, mothers would waken sleeping children with loud calls from kitchens warmly scented by fresh bread and coffee. In the bedrooms men would pull on pants, stagger to windows to breathe in the freshness of the morning air. The town would awaken into a new day, would follow the daily routines of life in all its simplicity and complexity until the people momentarily forgot the sufferings of their counterparts in the cities. And then night would fall, darkness would cover the mountain, and the planes would reappear in the distant sky.

Onward, in rhythmic repetition, flowed the days of the people of Careri, until one day, when a current of change surged its way through the hopeful, skeptical town. It began with announcements – deep, serious voices crackling through public speakers and radios, informing the people of Italy that in Rome an armistice had been signed. The townspeople soon learned that the government and military command had fled the Eternal City. Law and order departed. The country was left without leaders, the army abandoned.

Afterwards, it was said that many of the soldiers, dejected and fatigued, had thrown off their packs, their gear, their weapons, and took up the long trek to wherever home was. For weeks they walked, nocturnally, painfully aware of the threat of the partisans who remained hidden and active around them. All across Italy soldiers ambled beneath the darkened skies, along the moonlit roadsides, the coasts, the starlit crooked paths through countryside and meadows, while the hardware of warfare – hand grenades, rifles, machine guns – lay scattered where the men had dropped them. On the mountain, the guns of Careri were abandoned, their missiles piled high behind them, their guardians gone.

And while the soldiers of Italy were dispersing, spreading out and up and down the peninsula as individual men, the soldiers of Germany, properly formed in units, were following orders, conducting an orderly movement northward in trucks, cars, tanks, and motorcycles. Up from the deep south they came, moving away from the Allies, a sweep of military equipment surging forward towards Rome.

On the mountain, in the thick heat of the summer, the people of Careri watched the procession passing through their town. For seventeen days they watched. For seventeen days the soldiers of Germany moved through, their trucks and cars and tanks on a forward roll, their motorcycles riding back and forth, back and forth, their riders giving orders and relaying information in a language foreign to the townspeople. It was a terse language, sharp to their ears, and they despised the sound of it. They watched the giant tanks maneuvering through narrow streets, and curled their lips in disgust as the machines tore off sections of walls in their plowing, leaving crumbled stone and masonry behind. They watched with disdain and fear the retreating soldiers who plundered the towns and countryside, taking food, tools, livestock, anything at all without resistance.

But the fear of the soldiers was a rational fear, a fear that could be controlled by acquiescence. There remained a far darker dread for the townspeople. The war was nearing its end, yet in all the time it had been raging, only now, at its close and in seventeen endless days, did the townspeople come so close to knowing the true terror of death by violence. As the soldiers of Germany passed through the town of Careri, the airmen of England, two, three times a day, swooped down in their fighter planes to destroy them. The sound of the planes signaled the soldiers to dismount their cars and trucks and motorcycles, to take cover under the vehicles. Swiftly, and with precision, the planes zoomed low over the town, spattering machine gun fire through the streets before pulling upwards and away. The bullets did not distinguish between German soldiers and Italian townspeople. Both had their wounded, both had their dead.

At the end of seventeen days the last of the German tanks passed through the town and a quiet relief rippled among the townspeople. Their streets were grimy with dust and rubble and blood. They knew that the sound of machinegun fire would continue to echo through the still mountain air for some time as the airmen of England continued to follow and kill the soldiers of Germany on their northward march. And the townspeople would mourn for the dead even as they cared for the maimed, and never would they forget the sound of the bullets spitting death into their faces. But on that day, in the streets and *piazze*, in the homes and shops of Careri, a collective sigh like the first breath of life lifted gratefully into the summer air.

◊ ~♦~ ◊

The man of peace is a greater conqueror than the man of war, and a nobler one.

- Victor Hugo

◊ ~♦~ ◊

At Sea

C.R. Resetarits

Ten years past the Great War, Hubert is alone on the deck of a ship en route to another season's excavation at Ur. The moon overhead is new, buttery, rimmed in blue. Its light pours through the dark sky, falling iridescently weak upon the black Mediterranean Sea. For Hubert there is everywhere the sound of satin, in the sea rolling underneath, in the muffled turn of the ship's engines, in the shy "night-night" of his young bride sleeping below.

He can't quite believe he's taken her on. His marriage is as much of an arranged affair as deemed decent in modern times. It seems a reasonable solution. Marriage is, after all, a prerequisite to so many things, especially among their kind. Still, he can't quite fathom it. Thoughts of his bride leave him anxious and agitated. My work, he answers when she asks if anything's wrong. His work this year is pivotal. Absolutely. She'll need to be patient. The work is paramount. Besides, things between men and women usually worked themselves out over time, don't they?

His marriage certainly can't change the past, and it is the past that concerns Hubert most now. He has this season's exorcism to perform, his duty to the dead, his attempt to keep the past and present in proper place. He will stay on deck until his mind is scourged, until his war memories are, once again, renewed and packed away. Coleridge's mariner had that albatross trailing him at sea. Hubert has the war. His marriage can't change that.

Hubert feels it odd that he is haunted by memories of the siege of Kut only at sea. One would expect that the desert or the confines of the burial chambers at the Tel-sha-Annim dig would be more evocative, but he never thinks about the war or its terror once in country. One of many there: he is, the siege is, even the war. Great War indeed. How many great wars have been fought in Mesopotamia? Civilizations and alphabets, monsters and myths, gods and god-kings have battled in the region since the beginning of man. Perhaps it is the enormity of this perspective at the dig that keeps him free there of his own war memories. Or perhaps he remembers at sea because he feels safest, freest afloat.

It was at sea that he first admitted any recollection. During the siege, the surrender, and later as he fell ill in Baghdad, he had not allowed himself to register the events – not until the hospital ship he was put aboard reached the Arabian Sea did he begin to remember.

Bound for Bombay, for healing, memory, fear. As sick and stunned as he was in Kut and later in Baghdad, he was never afraid. Anxious, yes, always anxious and agitated, yet increasingly outgoing, chatty, expending too much time masterminding word games or pranks – anything other than wait – which was out of character for him. He was rarely so sociable. But, he'd refused to experience the terror that he'd seen on his men's faces, refused to subject them to a glimpse of their own doom in his own. Men braver and more attuned to reality than he, no doubt, but they were looking for fortification not empathy. No, not at Kut nor later in Baghdad.

In Baghdad he'd seen the damned, the already dead, walking along the Tigris. They were walking up river, and he was headed down. When he was among the wounded exchanged with the Turks, he allowed himself a bit of fear. Only a bit because behind the fear was a great wall of shame and wonder at being alive when so many were dead. No, it wasn't until the medic aboard the hospital ship at Basra brought him rum and milk that he finally fell apart. Besides, it was all a dream anyway, like an old Arabian tale. How could he have seen what he'd seen and yet live to drink rum and milk floating the while on the dazzling blues of the Arabian Sea? How could he be floating now across the Mediterranean toward that very same desert?

Yet he returns. Time and again, he returns: to the sea, to the baked sand of the dig, to uncovering the ruins of man.

A light blinks off the port bow. Shapes are emerging out of the sea: velvet to the satin. Are they the Greek Isles or sea sirens waking or, perhaps, the idea of his sleeping wife rising out of his own inky depths?

Should he go below and wake her? Wrap her in his mac and bring her on deck? Introduce her to the wonders of Mediterranean nights? Reenter the ancient world with his arms wrapped tightly around her next-to-nothing form, her compact gravity, the density of her looks of hope and care? He wants to move but can't. He's afraid of somehow giving himself away. But to whom, to what?

All around him shadows began to rise and fall as the steamer moves among the isles. He watches, remembers, desires, dreads. He thinks and then tries not to think of her. He tries to fortify himself against her with thoughts of duty and work, to cloak his siege craft in barbed-wire rings of benevolence, but he is, in this at least, anything but benevolent and she is everything but duty. She is a Trojan horse. She is Townshend sailing up the Tigris. She is a siren at sea, an angel's grace. She is a mug of rum and milk out on the Arabian Sea. She is there now, rising out of black waters, a shimmer, a threat, beckoning to break him down, to sabotage his long-held captivity.

◊ ~♦~ ◊

... life is a war, and a sojourn in a strange land, and fame after death is mere oblivion.

- Marcus Aurelius

◊ ~♦~ ◊

Chance of Rain

John Gifford

For thirty-nine days the temperature in the desert had peaked at one hundred and fifteen degrees. But on the fortieth day, clouds moved in and choked out the sunlight. The temperature struggled to reach ninety. That evening, the weatherman broadcasting on the Armed Forces Radio Network called for a fifty-percent chance of rain.

Through the door of the tent, Richard Juergens noticed lightning flashes in the sky. He and his machine gunner, Corporal Ramsey, were paired up against two other soldiers from the First Battalion in a game of spades. The men were sitting on cots inside the tent. Richard Juergens was about to throw down a card when the early-warning siren erupted. Lightning flashed in the sky. The lights in the tent blinked and then went out.

"Dude!" Ramsey said. "I had a good hand."

"Dude, get your gas mask on," Richard Juergens said. He removed his mask from the canvas pouch around his waist and pulled the straps over his head. With the rubber mask covering his face, he inhaled. Air rushed in through the filters. He felt the mask seal against his jawbone. "Got it on?" Ramsey didn't answer. He had run to the door. Richard Juergens saw him looking out into the night.

"Ramsey, quit screwing around and get your mask on."

"I don't have it."

"You better. You know you're not supposed to go anywhere without your mask and rifle."

"I left it in my tent. I didn't think I'd need it."

"Don't you take anything seriously?" He shouted to project his voice beyond the barrier of the gas mask. "That was an order from the colonel. And me."

Richard Juergens walked to the door where Ramsey was looking up into the sky. Soldiers were running back and forth in the corridor between the tents. The siren continued wailing. It reminded him of the tornado sirens that sounded each spring in Texas, and the noise gave him goose bumps on his neck and arms.

"Supply ships in port today," someone said. "That's why they're gunning for us."

Richard Juergens turned and walked back through the tent. He checked to make sure every man had his gas mask on. Then he turned back to Ramsey and said, "Come on. We're going to get your mask."

But before he was out the door, two explosions sounded, shaking the wooden frame of the tent. The noise reverberated through Richard Juergens' head, down his spine, rattling the fillings in his teeth.

"Patriots are up," someone else said. "That SCUD's headed our way."

"Everybody get down behind the sandbags and keep your heads down," Richard Juergens said. He looked back toward the door. In the illumination from a lightning flash, he saw Ramsey kneeling beside one of the cots. Ramsey's head was bowed and his hands were clasped together near his chin.

Just then a voice came over the loudspeaker outside, shouting *Gas, gas, gas! This is MOPP level three.*

Richard Juergens walked over to Ramsey and put a hand on his shoulder. He could feel the corporal shaking.

"I never got my anthrax shot!" he said.

"You're kidding me."

"I wish."

"You lied to me. You told me you got it. What's wrong with you?" Richard Juergens felt the acid boiling in his stomach. He could hear soldiers running outside the tent, their boots striking the ground, then kicking at the sandbags as they scrambled over the barricade. *Gas, gas, gas!* the voice continued over the loudspeaker. "Why didn't you get your shot? You knew this could happen."

"I was afraid of the side effects," he said. In the lightning flashes, Richard Juergens could see the sweat glistening on Ramsey's face. He could see the whites of his eyes glowing. His Adam's apple jiggled as he talked. "The corpsman said it's only been tested on cows. I ain't a damn cow! What if I get cancer or something?"

"What if you don't live long enough to get cancer?" Richard Juergens said. "We're going to go get your mask."

"I don't think we should risk it."

"You willing to bet the missile won't fall on us? You willing to bet it's not dirty?"

Ramsey, sitting on the edge of the cot, buried his face in his hands. The lightning flashed, and Richard Juergens saw the cards scattered on the plywood crate they had used for a table. Playing spades had been Ramsey's idea. Richard Juergens wasn't a gambler; he didn't even know how to play the game until Ramsey had taught him. He had told him they could win some money.

"I don't like to lose money," Richard Juergens had said.

"We have a good chance of winning," Ramsey had told him. "I feel good about it."

Now, listening to the sounds of the rain beginning to pelt the heavy canvas tent, peppering the sandbags on the bunker walls just outside the door, falling loudly, forcefully, inevitably, Richard Juergens closed his eyes and whispered a prayer behind the protection of the rubber mask that sealed his face from the elements.

Ramsey stood up from the cot and said, "I hate this. I hate not being able to do anything. I don't even want to think about what's going to happen if those Patriots miss and that SCUD hits us."

Richard Juergens broke the seal on his gas mask, pulled it from his head, and felt the air suddenly cool and refreshing on his face. With the mask off his face, his vision was clear and sharp.

"You better not think about it, then" he said. "Here. Put it on, and let's get down by those sandbags."

◊ ~♦~ ◊

War is not so much a matter of weapons as of money, for money furnishes the material for war.

- Thucydides

◊ ~♦~ ◊

A Deepening Heart

Thom Brucie

Often, during times of desperation, only his love for Miss Agnes Perser kept Nathan Branchwell on the right side of sanity, and one day, the Rev. Perser would give permission for Nathan to marry her. The more he missed Agnes, the more Nathan wished for the Civil War to end. The men had gone nearly five months without pay. Rations arrived with little regularity, and the soldiers began to spend more of their time and ammunition on rabbit and squirrel than on battle. Uniforms became torn, unwashed, and often devoid of rank or insignia. The men simply knew by face who was private, who was sergeant. This was the general condition of the men of the 110th Pennsylvania on the night of October 19th, 1864. They had been camped nearly four weeks near Kernstown, Virginia, and Nathan sat alone watching the jittery flametips of his fire. The quiet of darkness settled over him, and his thoughts slipped unexpectedly into a peacefulness he had not dared in years. The gurgle of the stream and the soft breeze rustling the grass soothed him. His breathing felt liquid and transparent, as if he were connected to the currents of water and the currents of air, and all the simple breaths he breathed reminded him of life and of growing things like hay and sunflowers in a garden.

Nathan reached the decision to join the volunteers after he spoke with the Reverend.

"I want to marry Miss Agnes," he said to the Rev. Perser.

"I can't allow it," the Reverend said.

"Why not?"

"It's the time, my boy. War. Uncertainty. I want my daughter to enjoy a comfortable home. You have no stake, Nathan. Nothing to offer."

"What can I do?"

"I don't know."

They stood quiet a moment. Then the Reverend mused. "Men honor gold," he said. "Whatever should happen, gold will last."

"Some men find their fortunes in war."

"Some men do, yes."

"I will."

Reverend Perser studied him.

"Please, sir."

"I cannot make such a decision for you, Nathan, but if you return from the war with gold enough to stock a young farm, I believe the good Lord will bless your efforts. With that, I would grant a union between you and my daughter."

Nathan accepted his admonition, and of those irregular times when the soldiers did receive their thirteen dollars in monthly pay, he traded his paper money for gold. He offered three times the face value of any gold coin. It was a time of general madness, so his mild idiosyncrasy caused little concern, and men sought him out, for three times the money meant three times the whiskey and sometimes a woman's favor. Over a period of three and a half years, Nathan traded for and saved two hundred dollars, four 50-dollar gold pieces.

How much would two hundred dollars buy at the end of the war? Nathan felt certain he could afford one milk cow, two Morgan horses, a double harness and a plow, a shovel, a hay fork, and all the seed for a first planting of beans, corn, and hay. Besides these he added a double-handled saw and two axes, one chopping and one finishing, so he could fell the trees and shape them into a two-room cabin. He was certain to find a down mattress, pots, kitchen utensils, and such cooking provisions as flour, lard, and salt to last the first year. Finally, with good neighbors, he would stand a barn of a weekend, pen in some chickens, fence in a hog, and still manage to bury two of the gold coins. Surely, the Reverend would honor his promise.

Suddenly, the gallop of a horse disturbed Nathan's reverie. He watched the rider kick the sides of the animal all the way to the Captain's tent. This bothered Nathan, because he respected animals and liked them. Since he cared for the stock, he knew the horse would be lathered and sore, and Nathan would be up late caring for it.

Captain Hollingsworth jumped from his chair, and the rider saluted. Nathan watched the men gesture, their arms and heads bobbing shadowy behind the glow of the Captain's fire. What news did this night rider bring?

Captain Hollingsworth commanded the 110th Pennsylvania. He had not distinguished himself in battle, but he courted power, and his commander, Colonel Geoffrey MacGeorge, was a man who remembered favors. Captain Hollingsworth spent much time cultivating the Colonel's ear, hoping that at war's end, the Colonel would reward him with the rank of Major. The Captain suspected that Washington and Richmond were close to resolving their differences, and he knew he needed one last opportunity to impress the colonel.

In the morning, word spread: a major battle, a decisive battle, perhaps a concluding battle threatened. No one knew specifics, but the rumors of war bring tension, and weary expectation mingled with the coffee and the talk.

Captain Hollingsworth called for the tracker, Manning, two sharpshooters, Steadman and French, and Nathan.

"Men, Colonel MacGeorge has put me in charge of a scouting party. We won't engage, just survey. I have a sense he'll reward any good news we bring him." Then he turned to Nathan. "Branchwell, I want you along to watch the stock in case of an injury. They must be ready for quick rides and hard terrain."

"What are we looking for, sir?" Manning asked.

"I don't know. And I don't know what we'll find." Before he dismissed them, he said, "Gather gear and supplies. We leave in two hours."

They took a southern tack, using the protection of forests along the hills. Late on the second afternoon, they rode into a tree-line where the air turned pungent.

"What's that smell?"

"Quiet," Hollingsworth said.

They slowed their pace, but the horses struggled against the reins. The men heard no unusual sound, but their ears strained in an effort to interpret the uneasiness they felt. Suddenly, they all stopped. Ahead of them, through the branches and leaves, they saw a battlefield, a small, unknown location, quiet and eerie with motionlessness. Captain Hollingsworth dismounted. He handed the reins to Nathan. The captain signaled the others to follow him. Each, in turn, slipped from the saddle and gave their reins to Nathan. Nathan pulled the horses together behind a tree.

"Shhhh. Shhhhhhh," he whispered.

The tree line followed the contour of the hillside opening to a small clearing with a stream which flowed away from them. Each man took a position crouched behind a tree. They waited, listening, watching for movement, but nothing moved, and no sound came from the field. Nathan kept the animals quiet, but they didn't like the acrid smell.

Manning circled left for half an hour. He found no signs of life.

Captain Hollingsworth panned the field with his looking glass again and again. Finally, he decided the meadow contained no threat, and he ordered the men out of the trees. Their senses remained alert, but even for these men who had come to know depravity, the stench and silence of this dead place restrained them. Their voices fell momentarily dry, like talcum. Death stretched before them without end. In the heat, bloated carrion stunk like vinegar. Cannons lay muzzle first into the mud. Ghostly bodies leaned as if asleep, and no one could distinguish blue uniform from gray. Their ears began to fill with a quiet buzz of flies – blowflies, horseflies, and blackflies, and at once the men recognized that the gray film which dulled the red earth was alive. They watched the hypnotic undulation of maggoty decay. Nathan huddled within the hot breath of the horses, and although flies found their salty hides, the horses, knowing Nathan, stayed calm. Minutes dragged with the miserable slowness of the sun, and nothing stirred – not squirrel, not rabbit, not man.

Hollingsworth turned his thoughts to the Colonel. How would he react to this event? It seemed final, as no battle before had felt. Hollingsworth knew he would have to find something exemplary for his report, but nothing exemplary remained among the carnage, only the pitiful silence of exhausted savagery.

Suddenly, a mule brayed. When they heard it, each man strained to determine its origin. Again, the pathetic bray sounded, painful and unhappy, and with it the sucking sound of a boot or a foot or a hoof pulling against mud.

"There," Nathan shouted, and he ran the twenty yards, jumping over cadavers and splintered trees to a muddy bank. The others followed to a low gully, the slow running water in its basin stained purple. A Confederate stamp on the mule's strap identified it. The mule looked young, recently pressed into service. The wide black eyes of the beast looked full of puzzlement.

"Help me get it to its feet," Nathan said.

"Wait," Captain Hollingsworth said. "It's a Reb. Leave it be."

"It's a mule," Nathan said.

"It's a Reb mule," the captain repeated.

"Let me save it."

Nathan reached for the rein and tugged, but the brute could only show its teeth and bray. Nathan struggled, but mud and exhaustion held the beast, and it would not stand. Nathan turned to the others. "Help me," he said.

Steadman and French moved to help.

"Stop," Hollingsworth said. "I said it's a Reb, and a Reb it stays." He drew his side arm and cocked the lever.

"It's not our enemy, Captain," Nathan said. "It's a mule, a live thing among all this dead."

"That's dangerous thinking, Branchwell. You should know better."

Hollingsworth pointed his pistol at the aggrieved animal, but Nathan stepped between them.

"I can't let you, sir. I can't."

"Don't make me shoot you over a dumb Reb mule. Step aside."

Nathan looked squarely into his commander's eyes. The Captain did not blink.

"I'm asking you not to shoot it," Nathan said.

"You or the mule," Hollingsworth answered.

Nathan clenched his teeth and decided to back away. As he took a step, Hollingsworth fired, and Nathan jumped. The bullet missed Nathan, but dirt sprayed onto his boots.

"Sir," French called. "Are you sure this is what you want?"

"He disobeyed an order."

"But, sir, it's Branchwell."

Nathan's nose flared, and he kept his eyes on the trickle of smoke that eased from the barrel of Hollingsworth's Colt, and for a moment, no one spoke.

Finally, Hollingsworth said, "Mount up. There's nothing to report here."

Nathan did not move. "What about the mule?"

Hollingsworth walked toward the horses. "Mount up," he said. As he swung into the saddle, he looked at French. "Shoot the Reb," he said.

"Wait," Nathan said. "I'll pay."

Hollingsworth reined his horse.

"There are four of you. I've saved four fifty-dollar gold pieces. If you help me with this mule and let me take him home, I'll give them to you. One for each."

"I'll take a gold piece over a dead mule any day," French said. "What's the loss if one Reb mule lives?"

Hollingsworth dismounted and nodded his chin in the direction of the mule.

Nathan leaned down and grabbed the mule's reins. The mule curled its lip, braying and jerking its head. Steadman and French pushed the haunches, forcing the animal to stand. Gray mud oozed under the shifted weight. A dank pool of dark water filled the hollow left by the emaciated body. Nathan motioned with his eyes, and Steadman unstrapped the broken supply baskets from the mule's back, leaving the tie straps. Nathan held the reins and whispered to it.

"Calm now. Calm," he said.

Manning pulled one hoof from the glue-like mud, and French pushed. The frightened mule lifted one leg, then another. Finally, it stood on firm ground.

Nathan found a wound at its rear leg near the stomach. He

thought the lead might have grazed the flesh and not entered it.

"It's free," Hollingsworth said. "Pay us."

Nathan examined their greedy eyes. As he reached for his pouch, he realized the cost of this mule – his gold, his farm, perhaps even his marriage. He could not renege. Even if he shot the mule himself, the others would take his gold. A battlefield oath cannot be undone.

The pouch felt heavy and full of promise. As he drew the strings apart, the men moved closer, every eye on the coins. One at a time, he paid their fee: Hollingsworth, Manning, Steadman, and French.

Nathan kept his original enlistment orders at the bottom of the pouch. After handing over the last gold piece, he removed the paper. It was creased and yellowed, but he had preserved it all these long years. To his own surprise, he tore the paper into small pieces and let them drop around his feet.

"We're done with this war," he said. He pulled the reins to lead the mule. "We're going home."

He moved to the horses, untied his haversack, grabbed his musket, and walked away. He headed north in search of water and perhaps some rest. He did not say good-bye, nor did he flinch when Hollingsworth called after him. Instead, he wondered if Miss Agnes Perser would consider one rebel mule wealth enough for marriage if the man who possessed it loved her.

The sun turned okra, and a thin twilight fog began to form. Nathan coaxed the mule with soft encouragement, even though the stout neck sagged and the eyes began to lose their glisten. Nathan tried to comfort the animal by rubbing its jaw and feeding it a hard-tack cracker. The wound bled again, but not seriously, Nathan judged. Still, a bleeding wound stirs concern. After perhaps two hours, he stopped at the top of a hill. They had traveled far enough from the slaughter to smell pine pitch, and the water in the stream ran clear over bluestone and pebbles. He could see the battlefield, but from a distance. The distance gave him courage enough to ignore it and to begin what might be called a healing as reality moved slightly toward memory.

They walked down into a green gully to camp. Nathan tied the reins to a rope, and he tied the rope to a tree so the animal could graze. The mule stood silent, as if it still carried supply boxes and it hadn't slept in a day or two.

Nathan boiled water for coffee. He did not eat. He rubbed his hands in the fire's warmth, and he wondered about the value of the mule, the gold it cost, and the queer decision to forsake the war. He imagined the conversation with his father. His father would say, "Brute appearance calls it foolhardy, but in ten years you'll know its value." Then Nathan imagined his father would return to his field work. Perhaps he would never speak of it again.

The loss of gold seemed fundamentally unsound. But what price a life? His mother, he knew, would value the life. Comfort, to her, came in a smile and a thankful embrace. She would be happy that Nathan returned home alive. Whether he returned with gold or with a mule she wouldn't care. But that's a mother's love; it holds no count in the business of men.

A breeze rustled the weeds, and Nathan finished the coffee with a gulp. He felt tired, and he began to ache in the way only a man who has escaped war can ache, bone-deep and permanent. He thought how the end of this journey would bring him home. Then he closed his eyes. He imagined that his father would stop his work to watch Nathan's approach. His mother would smile and wave and call his name. And he would see Agnes. As he thought of them together, he slept nearly four hours without waking.

When he did awaken, it took several seconds before he

remembered where he was and why. He turned to see the mule in the moonlight. He stirred the coals of the campfire, added broken twigs, and coaxed the weary embers back to flame. He went to the mule and stroked its mud-caked hide. "I'll rinse you in the daylight," he said. He looked across the back of the mule to the hill-line admiring the calm of the night-lit tips of high grass. It was the first time since leaving home he was alone. The mule brayed. The fire crackled. The night solitude carried the noises in echoes. He went to his bedroll and made a pipe.

The mule moved a little closer to the tree, but Nathan could not tell if it had grazed. Come light, he would hand feed it and bring it to the water for drink. Then he would wash the mud from it to begin its rejuvenation. He planned his route north, almost a straight walk, barring renegade militia and federal search parties. He would walk slow, stopping to rest the mule. He might need to work a day at a willing farm for food. Even under the worst scenario, he calculated he'd be home in three weeks. The thought of it made him smile. Home. Home and Agnes.

He slept again.

At dawn, the mule brayed and woke him. Nathan took the mule's bray as a good sign; perhaps it wanted water or feed. While the sun moved along the horizon, Nathan rose to attend the mule. He undid the rope to lead the animal to the stream. It brayed again, but Nathan shivered at the sorrowful sound.

"What?" he said to it, touching the jaw, patting the haunch. The eyes looked hollow and dry, beginning to turn opaque around the edges.

"You'll be fine," Nathan said. "Come on."

He tugged the rein. The mule trudged without resistance to water's edge, its ribs shadowy along its hide. It did not bend to drink. Nathan cupped a handful of water and rubbed it around the beast's lips and tongue. Droplets fell from its whiskers back into the stream, and the mule bent after them to drink.

Nathan patted its neck. "Good," he said.

Nathan bent too and rinsed his mouth. Then he drank.

He left the mule untied; it would not run. He went to the fire and added kindling and pinecones to the embers. He sat in the dewy sunrise, the smoke from the campfire a comfort of pine scent and ash. The mule moved warily to graze and chewed the grass more like a cow making cud than a horse-breed chewing feed, slow and repetitive, almost melancholic. He thought the mule looked haggard. Perhaps the emotion of the battlefield kept him from recognizing its state. Could it have been his frustration with death that led him to the reckless choice he now possessed? Why did he save the animal? Why did he pay such an awful price for its life? Surely, Agnes would ask him these very questions.

"Why, Nathan? What drove you?" she might ask.

He knew what he would tell her. One thing only drove him. Love. It felt like an incorrigible piece of knowledge, yet true and agreeable, like his love for her. He had to save the beast. It had survived the war, and Nathan knew it represented both his own survival and the survival of their love. That's what he would tell Agnes. He looked upon the sad, silent beast, and in that moment, he loved it – as a symbol, as a living thing, as a hope. Nathan drew on his pipe and exhaled a firm stream of smoke. He poured coffee into the metal cup and sipped gingerly allowing the heat and sour grounds to ease past his tongue. The warmth seeped into his stomach, and the heat of his belly and the heat of the cup against his hands warmed him.

The Rev. Perser would also ask Nathan about his decision. Rev. Perser was a man of principles, a godly man, a man obligated to rigid rules – the singular moralities of Christian faith and the simple exigency of money in a commercial economy. Would he accept love as an item of barter?

"Perhaps not," Nathan answered. "What then?" he asked into the steam of the cup. But he had no answer to that. Many rules die in war, and traditions too, but a daughter's responsibility to obey her father does not die. If Rev. Perser forbade Agnes's marriage because Nathan had no money, she would obey. What then would Nathan do?

The sun began to heat the air, and Nathan decided to break camp. Perhaps an answer would come to him. He doused the fire with the remaining coffee and took the pot and his cup to the stream to rinse them. He led the mule by the rope. After he washed the utensils, he drank again and splashed his face. When he rubbed his eyes clear, he realized the mule had not moved. Nathan went to it then and coaxed it to the edge of the water, but the mule struggled and halted at the mossy recession of the bank.

Nathan noticed the wound was bleeding again. He pulled the reluctant animal into the stream, and the water flowed around their legs in swirls. Nathan drenched his shirt and wiped the animal's wound clean. Then he washed the beast from head to haunch, dripping water back into the stream from its back and its legs. He cupped water to the mule's mouth and the wounded creature licked at it with its thick tongue, but it would not lower its head to drink on its own. It shook its muscles to remove the water from its hide, and droplets splashed Nathan's face and arms.

Nathan felt refreshed, almost invigorated. The chilly water cooled his skin and blood rushed pink under it. The mule stood in patient silence.

"All right, mule," Nathan said. "You're clean now. We can move on."

It's not a good idea to hike with wet feet inside wet boots, but

Nathan suffered an urge to keep moving. They progressed with slow steps, the sun ahead of them as they traveled easterly and north with the stream. The mule began to limp noticeably, and Nathan's feet began to rub against the sides of his boots.

"My toes are wrinkling," he said out loud. "We better make camp early."

He found a small area of brush and fallen leaves. Ferns and dark green bushes with tiny, white, star-shaped flowers made the place look restful. The stream hit a series of rocks and a slight drop in elevation caused the falling water to add a melody of comfort to the site. Nathan found a fire-site near two trees and a lichen-sided boulder.

He led the mule to some long grasses, but it did not eat. Nathan unstrapped the haversack and the Springfield. He took a paper plug and a pellet from the leather shot bag and loaded the musket.

"You might not be hungry," he said to the mule, "but I am. And I'm going to eat."

He patted the ribcage above the bleeding wound, turned, and walked into the trees to scare up dinner. The afternoon heat felt good on his tired muscles. He knew that the sun and a fire would dry his socks and his boots if he found dinner quickly. He came upon a decaying log, and when he kicked it, a rabbit jumped from underneath. Nathan fired quickly. The rabbit flipped once and dropped.

He lit the fire, skinned the rabbit and put it on a stick to let it skewer. He stretched his socks on a smooth stone and hung his boots upside down on two sticks near the fire.

He went to the mule. Its long ears hung like melting wax and its stubborn head fell, subdued.

"I'm sorry you got shot, mule."

He patted its neck. As he did, the scent of sizzling rabbit wafted into his nose. He inhaled deeply, allowing the green woods and the leaf mulch and the rabbit oil to fill his head.

"Some things are supposed to die, like that rabbit, so I can eat," he said. He grabbed the mule's ears, one in each hand. "And some things are supposed to live because they mean something. And you mean something. Do you hear?"

Nathan left the mule and strode to the fire. The tension in his stomach increased, but he confused uneasiness with hunger. He took some of the white corn meal from the flour sack, mixed water into it, and flattened the dough onto a fry pan.

"A corncake will taste good with rabbit."

Nathan turned the rabbit. Then he decided to turn his socks. They were beginning to dry, but the toes were stiff from the mud, so he had to rinse them again. He twisted each one, shook them, and replaced them on the warm stone. The corncake began to fry around the edges, and the rough doughy smell began to sweeten. He set the coffee pot to boil, and lit a pipe. He took a deep inhale and released the smoke up and away from his face. As he did so, a mosquito bit his skin and he slapped it and killed it. Its engorged belly splattered red. "Blood for blood," Nathan said and took his pipe again.

The comfort of the moment led his thoughts to Agnes, and he smiled. Somehow, he felt that she would understand his choice as a predilection in favor of life. He closed his eyes to see her, and she appeared as if real. Her long auburn hair surrounded her face and hung across both shoulders, straight and shiny like rippling water. Her brown eyes sparkled when she smiled, and he could see in them the fond yearning and youthful hopefulness that kept Nathan human during the muddy years of war.

"Will you marry me?" he asked.

"Will you marry me, Miss Agnes?"

"Agnes, will you marry me?"

He practiced the proposal so that when he asked in person she would have to say yes.

But the practice turned bitter as he imagined Agnes hesitating. "My father . . ."

The image collapsed, and Nathan opened his eyes to the hazy beginning of sunset and coffee boiling out of the pot. He pulled the pot away from the fire, shook the fry pan and leaned the rabbit higher to let the heat cook the inside meat more thoroughly.

Nathan tapped the ashes from his pipe, then poured hot coffee into his tin cup. He lifted a twig from the fire to re-light the pipe when the mule brayed. Nathan turned his head in time to watch the mule collapse awkwardly like a dog sitting on its own tail. He dropped the stick, put his pipe on the ground, and ran to the mule. Its legs were crumpled under its body, and its great head looked forlorn. Harsh breaths snorted from its nostrils. Blood oozed from the tiny wound at its side.

"You're going to die, aren't you?" Nathan said. He sat near its head and watched the ribs swell and fall in hard cadence.

"I can't save you, but you know I tried." Nathan looked away from the mule. "I can't do anything more," he said, his head still turned away from the great, round eye of the beast. When he turned back to the mule, Nathan realized suddenly that the long, black eyelashes made the thing look human, as if the eyes themselves could plead. Nathan exhaled. "I suppose there is one more thing I can do," he said. "I can make your passing easier."

Nathan went to his gear and brought the Colt .44 to the mule.

Nathan insisted that killing the mule constituted an act of love, an act internal and correct, a pitiful act of kindness in a harsh time – for where is the essence of a man if not in his capacity to love? He put the barrel into the mule's sad ear. "I love you," he whispered, and pulled the trigger. The gray sting of gunpowder burned his nose. He sat with the mule for a long time, until the smell of burning rabbit meat and overcooked corn meal reminded him of his surroundings and the other realities of his time.

He rose up then on his bare feet and walked to the fire. He took the burned rabbit and bit into the charred, ashen flesh. It tasted black and dry, and it satisfied his hunger deliciously. He flipped the burnt corncake into the fire, and the orange and blue flame that erupted from its center delighted him. He took another bite of rabbit and turned his face toward the motionless mule. He thought for a moment about the absence of gold with which he would return to Agnes, but he did not worry about it, for now he knew what he was capable of in the name of love, and Rev. Perser would know too, one way or another.

◊ ~♦~ ◊

Corn is the sinews of war.

- F. Rabelais

◊ ~♦~ ◊

Going Somewhere, or Coming Back?

Norah Piehl

We found him in Aisle 2, Bulk Foods, sheltered beneath the bins, as if he wished he, too, could dissolve, like rice or nuts, into a million tiny pieces. He lay on his side, knees jammed up to his chin, eyes screwed up, hands clapped fast over his ears. The only part of him not shut tight was his mouth, which was wide open; all right, gaping and uttering a low moan, words we couldn't understand.

Mrs. Kleinschmidt was just standing there over him, holding a plastic bag of trail mix by the wrong corner, so that each time she gestured an apology, M&Ms and peanuts clattered to the floor, two, three, a dozen at a time. She didn't seem to notice, but I sure did, surveying the hundreds of yogurt-covered raisins scattered all across the aisle. Those would be mine to clean up, later. But for now, according to Laura, my job was to get this guy out of Aisle 2, out of the store altogether if I could manage it.

"I sure am sorry, but I don't know quite what I did," Mrs. Kleinschmidt was saying to Greg, the security guy. "I just went down there to get my cart, and there he was, coming around the corner." She spoke more and more loudly to drown out the guy's drone. "I was startled, too, sure, but nothing like to how he was, you know. He just got real pale, dropped his basket, and ran away." I ventured down to the end of the aisle, and sure enough, there it was, upended, milk carton exploded, cans of soup and boxes of mac 'n' cheese soaked and ruined. It was going to be a long evening. "And then I came back here to tie up my bag, and he was already lying there like that," Mrs. Kleinschmidt went on, her gesture sending trail mix flying every which way, striking the plastic lids of the bulk food bins. I thought I saw the guy flinch a little.

Greg took Mrs. Kleinschmidt by the elbow, led her toward the exit, left me alone with the guy. I don't know why Laura thought I'd be the right person to deal with him. Sure, I was the maintenance girl, but I was supposed to pick up shopping carts from the parking lot, clean up exploding soda, smashed watermelon, toddler vomit in the cereal aisle. Not grown men shaking and cringing on the floor. Everyone in town knew about my family, though. Maybe that's why Laura thought I could get through to him.

I recognized him, of course; I'm sure we all did. It was late November, after all. This far north, once the summer cottages shut down, after the leaf peepers pass through, once deer hunting season is over, the only people left are the locals. Us, and the one or two clueless or crazy newcomers who choose to stick it out for the winter. They're the subject of speculation and endless gossip, the ones who keep ladies like Mrs. Kleinschmidt and my mom busy through the northern Minnesota winters, determined to figure out their stories before the spring thaw.

This guy had shown up in July, just like any other tourist, but instead of staying for a few days or a week, he rented the room over Mrs. Erickson's garage, settling in through fall. He didn't have a car or a job that we knew of. We saw him, most often, walking up and down the rocky beach or just sitting on the breakwall next to the lighthouse, surveying the lake as it evolved from blue and sparkling in August to gray and brooding in October. He was young, we thought, but looked older, his muscles knotty, his red beard long and tangled, speckled already with gray. Someone had heard that he was the oddball son of some businessman or politician who paid him to keep his distance. Mr. Blomquist said he was a brilliant but reclusive poet. But most everyone agreed that he'd been at war, one or the other of them, that his haunted eyes, scanning the lake, were seeing things none of the rest of us could, or would want to, see.

I tried to remember what it had been like with Tina, once we'd found her. We'd said so many wrong things that it was nearly impossible to remember what we'd gotten right. And that had been two years ago, when I was just a freshman, clueless about pretty much everything. "In her mind, she's still in danger," my dad had told me. "We need to remind her that she's safe."

So I sat down, right there on the aisle floor, within arm's length but not touching. He'd gotten quiet by then, so I just said, over and over, "You're OK. You're home. You're OK." For a long, long time, the only sound was the uncomfortable mashup of the peppy Muzak with the chorus of my low, slow chant and his dwindling moans. I don't know how long we sat there before his eyes opened, before he reached out for my hand with his trembling fingers. I looked up then, and saw Greg standing at the end of the aisle, holding back a crowd of curious but silent onlookers. Apparently the best show in Grand Marais that afternoon was at the IGA.

~

I didn't see the guy again for a couple of weeks. He'd left the store in a hurry that day, once he'd come back to himself, his groceries forgotten. But then, one unusually warm

Saturday in early December, foghorns woke me early. I had the morning shift at the store, so I decided to walk to work. I saw a figure sitting on a bench near the harbor. I wasn't sure it was him at first; details were blurry in the veiled early-morning light. I crunched my feet loudly on the frosty beach rocks as I approached the shore; I wanted to let him know I was coming, didn't want to risk startling him. I sat on a nearby bench, raised my hand in a wordless greeting when he glanced my way. He waved back, then stopped, hand suspended, casting his eyes away after he seemed to recognize me.

"Going somewhere, or coming back?" I asked, gesturing at the huge military-issue duffel bag slung on the seat next to him.

"Not sure yet," he said. "I'm a drifter, don't you know." His voice was soft, the vowels slow and creamy, Southern like sausage gravy. I glanced up, unsure if he was pulling my leg, saw a smile curve around the edges.

"I'm Sally," I said, half-waving again. A handshake seemed wrong somehow. I didn't want to remind him of that day, those awkward intimacies.

"Charles." He turned away, stared out at the lake, or where the lake would be once the fog rolled out. Mr. and Mrs. Lindstrom strolled by the shore with their springer spaniel, pausing for a time as if to zip up their fleece vests but really just taking stock.

"When I was growing up," he said softly as the Lindstroms walked off toward town, to their daily stop at World's Best Donuts, "there was this old guy. He'd just walk around town in his camo jacket, all day, like he was afraid to stop walking. We never saw him sit, or eat, or shit. We didn't know where he slept, if he even slept at all. Us kids had all these nicknames for him: G.I. Psycho, Loony Larry. Some kids yelled stuff at him, but mostly we just talked about him, imitated him, you know.

"One day he just snapped, I think. Stopped walking, finally, turned to a bunch of kids following him, acted like he had an invisible machine gun and was blowing them all away. Laughing all the time."

"But his was a different war, right?" I said. "A long time ago? Aren't things better now? At least a little? Can't you get help if you want it?" My words sounded foolish, even to me. Tina hadn't gotten any help until we'd seized it for her.

"It wasn't that long ago, Sally. Besides, all wars are the same, really, at least up here," Charles said, tapping his temple. "And crazy is as crazy does, right? Guess I'm scared I'm turning into him, that people like that" – he gestured toward where the Lindstroms had been a moment before – "call me Crazy Charlie or something."

I gazed down at my hands, remembering the thoughtless things I'd heard a couple people say after that afternoon at the IGA.

"And then one winter," the guy went on gently, "Loony Larry just vanished. Us kids were never sure if he got sent to a hospital or if he killed himself or what." He bent down to pick up a rock by his feet, rubbing his thumb rhythmically over its smooth blue-gray surface. "Lately I've been wondering if he just moved, kept walking all the way to Atlanta or New Orleans, somewhere he could just blend in. Where he wouldn't have been the craziest thing going. I get that, you know?"

I nodded, searching around my own feet for a perfect skipping stone. Round and flat, fitting easy into the curve of my gloved hand, begging to be hurled back into the frigid lake for a time. "My sister, Tina, was a combat medic in Iraq," I told him. "We still don't know everything that happened to her company, but she was pretty messed up when she got back. Then she just left. Disappeared. My mom and dad spent most of a year searching, until they found her on the streets in Minneapolis."

"Where she could just blend in," Charles said.

"I guess so. Anyway, my parents brought her back up here, even though she was embarrassed. Even though her boyfriend had married another girl while she was away. Even though the last thing she wanted, then, was to be home."

"Home," Charles repeated. "You kept saying that, that day."

"Well, it was, you know? And still is, for her, and could be for you too, I bet."

"So she's still here now?" Charles looked at me, surprised.

"Yeah – the Blomquists found her a job over at the nursing home. Just a physician's assistant thing, for now, until she's ready for more. But she's got that, and she takes swimming lessons at the Y every week, and she even teaches Sunday School. Hard to believe, but there it is."

Charles stood up, stone in hand, walked to the water's edge. I followed more gingerly – the air was cooling off, and the mist was settling on the beach, setting up a sheen of ice that made walking treacherous.

He sent his stone flying, straight and low, kissing the lake a half-dozen times at least before succumbing to its watery allure. "Our stone-skipping days are numbered, I think, at least for this year," I said, my own rock skipping a path just as long before its gray was swallowed by the lake's. "Although punching holes in harbor ice has its own sort of charm."

I paused, thinking about what needed to be said. "People truly want to help you, too, you know. They just don't know how to start. Like the Lindstroms, the ones who walked by before? They train service dogs for vets, dogs who could help you, let you know when Mrs. Kleinschmidt or someone is planning a sneak attack in Aisle 2.

"And I know Mr. Koski mentioned finding you a job at the public library. Just a few hours a week, you know, shelving, but still. He thought you might enjoy it."

"Seeing as I'm a brilliant but reclusive poet and all," Charles said, grinning a little, pushing back his too-long bangs with his bare fingers, turning purple with cold. "Or so they say."

"If we can't dig up a good story, we just make it up instead."

"I just don't know if I can handle being so . . . *seen*, you know?" Charles jammed his hands in the armpits of his canvas coat. I wondered if he owned gloves.

"Yeah, but you need to ask yourself – is it worse to be seen? Or not to be?" I checked my watch. "Damn – I'm going to be late for work. See you around?"

~

He didn't answer, then, just stood staring out across the horizon again, seeming to consider simply swimming to the other side. I waved a silent goodbye, walked toward the IGA. Before I got too far out of sight, though, I glanced back. The fog was lifting. Charles had picked up his duffel bag and was striding toward town, his silhouette brittle against the icy-blue sky, the color of winter.

Maybe he was just hightailing it to the first Arrowhead bus south to Duluth. Or maybe, I hoped, he'd make his way to

World's Best Donuts, warm his hands against a mug of coffee. One bite of their sugar raised, and anyone would find a way to stay a while.

◊ ~♦~ ◊

War is magnificent to those who never tried it.

- An old saying

O, withered is the garland of the war!

- Shakespeare

◊ ~♦~ ◊

The Consequent Phrase of a Melody

Margaret Kingsbury

The sky is a piercing clear blue, compelling her to stare upwards, searching, eyes watering with strain. She is a thin scarecrow of a woman with straw hair tightly restrained behind her head and premature lines marring her young and once fresh face. The biting, cold wind whips around her, burning her cheeks and ears and flattening her second-hand coat against her scrawny form – but still she watches the sky, intent. The animal screams of the children eventually break her concentration and she turns to them, frowning.

"Why aren't you two in the car yet?" she says, an edge in her voice belying her quiet tone as her eyes dart from each flushed young face.

"Mom, Shelia is *cheating!* It's not fair!"

"Nu-ah. Not a cheater."

The two children push each other, faces contorted into tight grimaces, teeth bared.

"Get in the car both of you, now."

The mother pushes the scuffling children to the old gray Honda that leaks life in an oily slime onto the concrete driveway. Picking up the youngest and opening the door, she places the squirming three-year-old into her car seat and forces the belt closed with a firm click. The child lets out one piercing shriek then quiets as the mother hands her a bag of gummy worms from the floor of the car.

"I call shotgun!" the son yells, running to the front of the car and hopping into the passenger seat with seatbelt clicked shut before the mother can protest.

"Charles," she sighs, her breath a puff of vaporized air in the frigid afternoon. The mother climbs into the driver's seat, brow creased in worry, and puts the keys into the ignition with a silent plea. The car jerks to a start and she smiles.

"Yeah! The car started!" the son says with a laugh, clicking on the radio and turning to his favorite station – the only station he listens to since his father left.

"This is NPR speaking with our correspondent in Haiti. Tell me, Emmanuel, how are the Haitian people dealing psychologically with such devastating losses?"

"Better than one would believe, Katie. Most simply want to move on with their lives and begin again, but with the devastated infrastructure . . ."

"Is Dad in Haiti, Mom?"

The mother carefully weaves her way through the traffic, imagining with every passing car a potential wreck that will cause the airbags to go off and decapitate her oldest child. She should not have let him sit in the passenger seat. She should have made him sit in the back.

"Mom?"

Her voice is tight with stress when she answers. "No dear; he's in Afghanistan."

She had told him this many times, but the child assumed whenever he heard a news report that it referred to his father.

"I bet he goes to help those people. Hey, do you think Dad will know who Shelia is?"

She glances in the rearview mirror at Shelia sleeping, a gummy worm clenched protectively in her fist.

"Of course he will."

"Oh, I guess you're right. She'll be with me. Hey, I bet

when Dad gets home . . ."

His voice and the news mix as the mother creates a fairy tale.

Once upon a time in a land far, far away, a woman lived all by herself. She was beloved by the entire village for her beauty and grace, but most of all for the fair melodies she created on the violin . . .

"Sixteen die in a suicide bombing in Pakistan while attending services at a local mosque . . ."

"And then I can show him my, um, new DS game, you know, the one that . . ."

Then one day a man came from a distant town, different from the other men in the small village. He carried a pipe that played lovely, bewitching music which cast a spell upon her, entangling her heart with his. His music was so bewitching she forgot how to play her own, and her violin was used instead as wood for the fire.

"Whoa, look at that car Mom! I bet Dad's never seen a car like that before."

". . . volcanic ash disrupting air travel across Europe . . ."

At the height of their romance, when she had bestowed to the man all of herself, a lion visited their cottage and carried the man away in its jaws, two specks of the man's blood dripping to the floor. Two changeling children sprang from the drops of blood, demanding the woman play the violin for them, but she no longer had a violin to play; she no longer knew her own melody, so they would not leave . . .

"Can I get a candy bar at the store Mom? *Please?*"

"A meteor lit up the sky above the mid-west yesterday, though scientists have yet to clarify the precise nature of . . ."

"Mom! I said PLEASE!"

"Give me some peace and quiet Charles, NOW!"

She clicks the radio off as she pulls into Kroger, parking between two great white trucks, half-hoping they would swallow the primordial Honda. Silence fills the car and she turns to her changeling son, who sits red-faced with crossed arms and furrowed brow.

"I'm sorry for yelling," she says.

"Dad wouldn't yell if he were here."

"Yeah, well your father left us. Now, will you please just cooperate and get out of the car?"

"He would buy me a candy bar too."

"Fine, you can have your candy bar, but only if you don't fight with your sister in the store. Deal?"

The son pushes the door open and jumps onto the pavement, slamming the door shut and awakening Shelia, who begins whimpering. The mother sighs and quickly exits the car.

"Stay with me, Charles. Don't go into the road by yourself."

"I can go wherever I want to!" the son says, but he stays by the car and the mother hurriedly unbuckles the whimpering Shelia, who still clutches the gummy worm in her fist.

"Let go, sweetie; let Mommy have the gummy worm." She crouches down and rests Shelia on her bent knees, gently prying her sweet, sticky fingers open.

"Here, let me." The son forces Shelia's hand open and the gummy worm falls to the pavement, Shelia shrieking and kicking in her mother's arms.

"No candy bar for you!"

The mother stands and slams the door shut, taking Charles' hand with her free one and forcing the two struggling, shrieking children into the grocery store, admiring their dissonant chords. She must make this fast. A smile tightens across her face as she passes other customers, who give her varying looks from disgust to pity.

"We're just going to pick up a pizza for tonight, Shelia; we'll be home soon."

The mother makes her way to the frozen food section, singing bits of vaguely remembered songs to try to calm the children. She searches and grabs the cheapest pizza, both children finally quieting from either exhaustion or the mother's aimless singing. She makes her way to the checkout, Charles lingering behind her.

"Hurry up, Charles; come here."

He obeys but begins rummaging through the candy bars by the checkout lane, sulkily touching each bar and moving them back and forth.

"No candy bar Charles – up here with me."

He looks sidelong at his mother and begins dropping bars onto the floor.

"Charles!"

The mother makes her way to him, her hands holding Shelia and the pizza, quivering in anger. She sets the pizza on the floor and bends over her son.

"No!"

She grabs his hand and slaps it – hard – his small hand turning red in hers. Sheila stares up into her face with wide eyes. She hears a woman whisper loudly behind her: "God, it's *those* kind of people who shouldn't have kids." The mother looks in the direction of the whisper and sees a girl probably her own age dressed in tight black skinny jeans and a purple peacoat, standing with an even skinnier and younger man wearing similarly tight jeans. The girl sneers at the mother as they make eye contact. *If I didn't have the children with me, I'd slap her small narrow-minded face, the bitch.* Picking up a candy bar and setting it on the belt with the pizza, she shoves the remaining bars into an empty box and stands, Shelia tightly wrapped around her left hip and sucking her thumb. The mother glances down at Charles, who is eagerly eyeing the candy bar.

"Your total is $14.72."

She digs through her purse for her credit card and hands it to the cashier, picking up her bag. The cashier hands her receipt and card back and the mother places them inside her purse, looking down and finding with a jolt of panic that Charles is no longer with her. Searching with narrowed eyes, she begins pacing the front of the store, heart hammering in discord. *Where could he be? Why does he have to wander off? I hate doing this alone. I hope he isn't bothering anyone. I hope he hasn't run outside, where a car could hit him.* She spots him by the sliding doors in front of a lottery ticket machine, its light casting a green tint across his smiling face.

"Can I get one Mom, please?"

The mother peers down at his green face with relief.

"Never do that to me again, Charles. You stay right by me, do you hear?"

"Alright Mom, I promise. I didn't mean to worry you. But look, they're only a dollar!"

She digs a dollar from her purse and hands it to him, smiling as he hastily takes it and slides it into the machine, pressing the lucky number seven button. The machine hums and spits out a ticket and the son gently lifts it from the machine door, holding it reverently in the palms of his hands.

"Do you think it's a winner?" he whispers, staring down into his hand, mouth forming a small O in wonder.

"You're the winner. Now come on to the car; if you sit in the back seat with your sister, I'll give you a quarter to scratch off the numbers." They make their way to the car, Charles chanting "Winner, Winner" to Shelia, who quickly begins mimicking her brother. Tucking them into the backseat, the mother hands the son a quarter and gets into the car. He begins scratching at the card, bits of lint flying onto his lap.

"Five dollars! Mom, I won five dollars!" he says, face wide and eager.

"Good for you! I knew you were a winner!" She carefully slides the keys into the car and turns, only to hear the scratching of the engine resisting.

"Can I go get my money now Mom, *please*?"

"Not today son, but next time we go to the grocery store." She quietly pleads with the car as she turns the key again and again.

"Come on, please. PLEASE."

"Why don't you wait? You can plan what you'll buy with it. It'll give you something to look forward to."

The engine starts. *Mommy's a winner, too.*

"I think I will buy more tickets – and candy bars. I bet Dad will win the war; he's a winner like me."

"I bet you're right."

The three make their way home, Charles and Sheila chanting "Winner, Winner" while the mother thinks of her husband, his long stern face that would turn into deep dimples and bubbling laughter in an instant. The way he sought her out after her first solo performance in the college orchestra, insisting she allow him to take her to dinner, eyes pleading with hers in an intensity that she now knows well. He was a man of many moods, like his son, and she longs for his return, for his sweet spell to come over her once again.

~

That night the mother crawls into bed, careful not to wake the two sleeping children who nestle closer, drawn to her warmth. One bedroom light remains on and fills the room with a gentle quiet light, protecting the children – and maybe the mother a little too – from the demons that hide in the dark. She insists the children sleep with her at night, missing the hard sinewy protection of her husband and detesting the thought of being alone. With a tender hand she pulls the covers up where the children have kicked them off, tucking the corners against the children's bony bodies. She misses him so much. She closes her eyes, leaning against the pillows and letting the night's melody fill her body: the caressing wind stirring the trees, the gentle glow of the bedroom light, the sharp cold emanating from the windows. Her breathing slows and she feels a peace enter her soul.

"Please" she whispers into the night, "Please bring him home." And she feels God answer in that caressing wind and sharp cold. For the first time since her husband's departure, she falls asleep without crying, but instead with a calm knowing smile soft on her face, a confidence in her soul that she has not felt since the days she played violin. But this time the music is different – quieter yet more intense. She is unsurprised the next morning when she is awakened with a phone call informing her of her husband's return. She is told that he will be arriving at the airport in two days; he is returning early from his post due to unforeseen complications.

"What sort of complications? He's not hurt, is he?" she questions, wondering at what price her plea would be answered.

"Well, ma'am, not physically, but you should be prepared. He's been having some suicidal tendencies, and the psychiatrists think he should come back to the states. I'm sure he'll be better once he gets home, ma'am, back to his family."

"Thank you. What time will his plane arrive?"

"0-700, ma'am."

"Thank you." She hangs up the phone, staring through the window at the overcast sky. "Please, let him be okay," she whispers into the dull gray morning, knowing that she has already asked too much, knowing that she will not be answered again. She breathes deeply and calmly, filling her lungs with air. She can hear the children stir in the bedroom, so she goes into the kitchen to start breakfast, humming a tune under her breath. She will take care of them. She will care for them all.

◊ ~♦~ ◊

The angel Pity shuns the walks of War.

- Erasmus Darwin

◊ ~♦~ ◊

◊ ~◆~ ◊

Arms maintain peace.

- An old saying

If we conquer our enemies by honest dealings and just treatment, our success is greater and more permanent than if we defeated them in war.

- Polybius

To brave men the prizes that war offers are liberty and fame.

- Lycurgus

◊ ~◆~ ◊

I Dream My Brother Plays Baseball

Lisa L. Siedlarz

On the field your platoon strategizes while Afghani
wind blows sand faster than Nolan Ryan's fastball,
blurring vision like rosin in a pitcher's eye. It sticks,
stings as bad as the last time I saw you at Ft Bragg,
a send-off for your twelve month mission.

From the stands I squint to see you as if I'd left my
glasses home. Bases and mound surrounded by dirt,
rocks, I turn and turn in this grey and translucent
gathering of blurred faces & monochromatic baseball
caps – *Do you see my brother? Can you see him?*

The crowd jumps up and roars as a soldier rips
a line drive through the gap, slides head first
into second just beneath the tag. A mailman
whose USPS eagle decorates his shoulders
like your army stripes, chases the play, throws

up his right arm to indicate safe. Under his left arm
he carries the package I sent to you a month ago,
labeled: If undeliverable, return to sender.
I take the box from him, hoping to hand-deliver
sunscreen, foot powder, Crystal Lite on the Go.

BATTLE RUNES

With my arms full, I run bases calling your name.
Rounding third, white-faced hornets block the way
home, the nest hidden in surrounding caves.

Insurgent Injured in Rollover
My Brother's Photo Series

He is strapped to the table,
a thick olive belt cinching
white swaddle. Blood leaches
below his knees, but the units'
attention is to his head
obscured by a neck brace.

Six men and a woman circle
with tubes, IVs, needles.
He reaches for my brother's
hand. Kevin clasps back, blue
latex against skin a comfort since
he can't understand a word.

The Afghan's grasp gives,
my brother rests his hand
on the table, moves to his head
to work a breathing bag, one breath
every five seconds:

one-one thousand one . . .

A medic starts compressions;
another preps a finger long needle,
injected into the IV, then his heart.
Defibrillator paddles are prepped,
pressed to the chest and bruised ribs.

The man's torso rises. I imagine
a whorl of murmurs and light
as he tries to read the relief
when my brother hears his heart
thrum in the stethoscope, says,
we got him back.

Who is She?

The Pashtun girl looks three maybe four. She wears
an emerald tulle dress. A lace collar, like doilies
my grandmother made, drapes her shoulders and chest.
Her neck is thin as a featherless bird's, tendons and blue

veins stick out from taut skin. Her head challenges
the grace of her neck, so she leans into her father
who stares down at her willing her to breathe. Breathe.
Her black eyes are turned inward, away from the endless

dust, endless echoes of gunshots and explosions.

She was ten, my brother says, *just stopped eating.*
He shakes his head. *Lost her will.* I look into her eyes
see how she turns in and in until she is weightless.
Blossoming into wings, did she rise up with the wind?

Commendations

The photos were kind: You, thumbs up in a shaded turret;
leaning against a truck wearing shorts and sneakers;
your bunkmate making animals out of balloons.
Vacation shots.

Aerials of mountains and sunsets,
camels drinking from a stream gave no warning
you'd come home clenching your jaw,
temper short as a fire ant.

When your tour ends, you show me how you earned
the Navy Achievement medal as a combat life saver,
Army Commendation medal as turret gunner, an ambush
 with a: *high rate of accurate fire ensuring safe passage*

the Kill Zone.

Awards commend your ability to stay calm
while *engaging the enemy, stabilizing critically wounded.*

Your commander calls you: *Mortar Medic Man Extraordinaire.*
You don't talk about ISAF operations,
or fire support against insurgents.

I look at the pictures you've brought home,
think: My god, this is a man's tibia. *Where's his foot?*
You shrug, *Still in the traffic circle. Twenty eight casualties that day.*
As if we're talking weather.

How the calf resembles tenderloin.
Here you bandage a leg while medics intubate
this man with a charred face. *Is he alive?*
Oh yes, you say, *but didn't make it.*

Then this one. You surrounded by eight boys
with bicycles and soccer balls,
everyone smiling, all dimples and teeth.

Trauma

*Wakey, wakey boyzz — someone mixed it up
with Hajji and we got some casualties.*

BATTLE RUNES

Sarge rips open blinds, I cram my feet
into gritty socks and boots, stumble
to the humvee that jolts us to the landing

where an ISAF chopper whines down
and NATO boys unload stretchers.

We jump to work. Danks, Mo and Dr. Jeebs
make for the head wound while 'scusees
bring us up to date: scouting mission ambushed
by an RPG, five casualties, two civilian.
Air strikes disintegrated their attack.

Strickland and Maz grab the Terp with
a shrapnelled leg. Elliot grabs the dude
with a burnt face. Me and Lev's guys –
arms and legs bandaged and bleeding.
I check vitals, hook 'em up with I.V.

We rock and roll to the aid station.
Just three trauma bays, a tent over gravel
a holding site. I ain't no doctor
but I know this dude is scared. I wet
a towel, pat down his forehead and cheeks.

Don't worry. You're with the Sand Sharks.
Pros doing what pros do.

Out the back door, the sky is devastatingly blue
If it weren't for the slash of mountains

you'd think it was water.
I grab scissors, prepare to cut away.

ATF Love

Anti Taliban Forces are the most macho
fighters we know. And the gayest.
These dudes, who carved up Russians
with bayonets, who ride three men

on a Honda 125 bike while on patrol,
slaughter Al Qaeda with grenades
and AK-47s, then kick back and listen
to love songs while holding hands.

Women are for children, men for love.
We laugh, call them the *Butt-Pirate Army*.
In our free time, we hang out at their posts,
play cards and watch Van Damme movies.

At night, these ATFs loiter on their small,
meticulously kept lawn lit by lamps made
from old Soviet bomb casings stuck
in the ground and strung with colorful lights.

Arms draped over shoulders and guns, they
sway to music from a boombox. Sometimes

they hire young teen boys to dance and sing
while bearded men with craggy smiles gaze on.

Later, we head back to our fort, where we sit
on upturned crates while wind fondles Shit lagoon.

Camels

Habibs keep them like pets. Nasty
split-lipped spitsters, the only thing
they're good for is the hair. Blankets,
clothes, tents, even twine.

They say the milk is good for us, sickly
sweet, watery, I'd rather drink black coffee.
Even the meat is tough and stringy.
Dung? Burn it for fuel.

I've watched a bull-calf follow this boy
for three days. An average life-span of forty
years, it's likely they'll be buried together.
Ata Allah, they say, gifts from God.

LISA L. SIEDLARZ

Don't Paint in Camels

Amazing creatures, really. The color of
heaped dunes, scorch just rolls over them.

I've marched their waveless beach, mirages
of smiles disarming and deadly. Those camels

marched knock-kneed and steady. Even under fire

they did not flinch. The mind is treacherous.

I see camels in stitches of multi-colored coats and falling
                                                                   foliage.
In burning bushes of autumn, red is an exploding oil well,

black clouds, souls of those who will never come home.
I'm fine now. I know I'm home when I hold my paint brush

and canvas, a good bottle of wine. I listen to the ocean's
music, become grounded. I will not drown in the legs

of this merlot. Will capture spray of ocean on rocks,
paint a picture of a life not mine.

Bury me in the sand and I will envy how clouds move on
like breath. Cold doesn't faze me, having walked

through dust-deviling hell where thoughts of winter saved
me from suffocation. Here I sit on this beach, sand

slipping through my open fingers to reunite with kin.
Sand is color-blind. Drinks blood as if it were water.

Mission Accomplished

I stepped on a booby trapped mortar
got blown into the air, weightless
until I thumped into the crater
gouged from the earth.

I was mystified, then saw my bunkmate's
face, eyes like full moons behind clouds,
how he repeated 'shit' like a worn
needle on a scratched vinyl forty-five.

I blacked out, woke up with my left leg
gone. Four months later, I played golf.
18 holes. Had to use a cart, but still.
Eighteen holes.

◊ ~♦~ ◊

The Death of a Phoenix

Dawn Sandahl

Wally was in his time of death. He knew it the way a man knows his lover is lying to him. That sudden ease, that big game. All the cards shown at once. He had stopped believing in the stories of the phoenix, the rising, the healing and all of that.

He discussed it all with Lewis, his cellmate. They liked them to call each other roommates, but they knew what they were. There was no use in obscure language.

Lewis the Explorer, Wally called him. Lewis talked to him about lightning the way Jesus would, about silence like a prophet, about life like a martyr.

For a long time, Wally listened. He only made cricket sounds when Lewis was talking. Wally felt like the tympanum of a drum feeding off of his vibrations. He had believed Lewis until he started talking about the phoenix. That's when he knew Lewis was crazy. Lewis the Explorer spoke a language no one else did, and for years Wally thought he could translate it.

~

"Wally," Sarah said. She was visiting for the first time in a long time and her eyes were soft. Her hair was different. Her wedding ring gone.

"What," he said with a mouth full of smoke. He let it trail out of his nostrils like a dragon's breath. Sarah spoke flowers like a field of wild blooms.

"Mom is not getting any better. She said she wants to see

you. I do, too."

He was silent for long seconds, letting the nicotine throb in his lungs for a moment. He'd stolen this cigarette from a nurse and needed to make it last.

"Wally," Sarah continued, "this place is voluntary. You can leave and come back."

"No. No, I'm not well."

"I see that." She pointed at the cigarette. "Should you be smoking in here?"

"I don't know what 'should' means," he replied. "I guess it's against their rules if that's what you are talking about. They don't let us have any of the comforts of our . . . *former lives*."

"Jesus Christ, Wally! It's a mental institution. You probably–"

He put his finger to his lips in a mock demonstration and said, "Shh, shh, shh. No foul language." He looked behind his shoulder as if he was expecting a nurse to be there. The visiting room was empty. "And don't even think about masturbating, or talking, or wanting to read a book, or taking a fucking crap whenever you feel like it, anything that might let them know you're a goddamn human. They'll strap you down and put some sleepy juice in your arm."

Sarah's hands curled and fidgeted on the table, which made Wally think of a dying spider's legs. "Will you please come home? If it's so bad, just check out of here."

He put the cigarette out on the stainless steel table between them. "No. I can't."

"Mom is dying, Wally. Don't you know that? Don't you even care about us?"

"No," he said. "Not anymore."

Sarah leaned forward and Wally could see new lines on his

sister's face. Her voice changed. It was quiet and small. "Do you remember the day on that bronze bus? Bus 105?"

"You know . . ." He chuckled and rolled his eyes to the ceiling. "You know that all life forms are really just balls of atoms and when we die our atoms will just be somewhere else? Lewis the Explorer told me that. He has been to all areas in the world and he's seen people die before. Up close. He's seen the atoms. He's seen the phoenix."

"Wally, I'm talking to you about the bus. Do you remember that day?"

Wally laughed and scratched his greasy hair. "I remember Lewis saying that we could all heal ourselves on an atomic level and just keep on living." Wally frowned, ready to cry. He slammed his fist on the metal table. "I don't believe it anymore. I don't believe it anymore, Sarah!"

Sarah looked at her brother's face. His eyes remained on her hands, never her eyes.

"Will you come home?" she asked. "Will you see Mom?"

"No."

"Do you care about us at all?"

"No."

She spoke slowly and with none of her previous kindness. "This is the last time I ever see you." She stood and walked out.

He was alone, but it was good being alone. He didn't have to pretend to know what anyone was talking about. He didn't have to be someone's vision of Old Wally.

He stood up and left to find Lewis the Explorer to hear some of his prophecy, leaving the smoldering cigarette butt on the table behind him.

~

This man looked like my brother. He *was* him in the sense that it was the same body and the same brain that had been alive for forty-four years. To the extent that all of us are the same person because of an uninterrupted consciousness of memories and experiences, my brother Wally was gone.

As I stepped out of the institution and into the February air with hot tears on my cold cheeks, the crisp air brought back a twenty-year-old memory of Wally and me at the bus memorial in downtown Chicago. We were best friends. I was twenty-one years old and Wally was just about to be drafted.

I was living with my first boyfriend Brian in his downtown Chicago apartment. My parents had always lived in the suburbs and I liked saying I was from the city. I liked taking the el train to Michigan Ave. and walking along the river, right next to people whose names were on bylines and book jackets and news programs.

Wally came to visit almost every day that fall and winter, ever since he'd gotten the letter from the government saying he had to serve. He'd quit his job at Kinko's and was blowing whatever meager savings he had on "living it large" for a while.

I wasn't working, either. The depression was horrible in 2019. Nobody talked about 1929 anymore. People thought breadlines were a thing of the past, but with just about everybody on food stamps, myself included, the budget cuts to the program reduced me to a diet of starch, fat, and salt. Brian let me stay with him for free, as long as I did the cooking and cleaning, the petty maintenance of life that he was not interested in. Wally spent most days with me, our heads hanging down, looking at our feet and telling each other things we had never known the words to say.

I stole someone's credit card to get the food for Brian's birthday. He said he missed steak. His parents bought it when he was a kid. It was just too expensive now. After I got home, I also ordered a shirt online for him.

That was a bad idea. I had a video message waiting to be opened on my computer as soon as I had ordered the shirt. I clicked on the icon for the message before I thought about it. Stupid IP address tracers. I knew I shouldn't have ordered anything online with the stolen card.

Two bejeweled, hair-sprayed middle-agers that I recognized from the el train were poking their faces amateurishly at the camera on their monitor. I saw a gazillion-gallon exotic fish tank burbling behind them. "We know that you have our credit card," the woman said. "Cut it up in front of your screen and we won't press charges."

I knew she had already seen me through the screen. It was too late to hang up. Besides, she had my IP address. Brian's IP address. I decided to be honest. "I made charges on it . . ."

The woman laughed. "It was only two-hundred dollars! Just destroy it in front of your monitor so we can be done with you."

"Sorry," I muttered and chopped the card in half with a pair of kitchen shears.

"Good," she said. "It'll take a day to be cancelled. If it is used again, you'll be hearing from us." She smiled and her husband nodded. "And the police," he added. Then, they ended transmission and I was alone again.

Brian arrived home two hours late, so the steaks – New York Strips – were cold and rubbery. They were marbled with too much fat anyway.

"Hi," Brian said in a breath that smelled like whiskey.

"I made you steak."

"Oh," he said and threw his briefcase onto the bed without seeing the silk rose petals I'd scattered there. "Probably shouldn't waste my money like that, you know."

"Well actually . . ." I decided to drop it. "You're late."

Brian frowned at me and turned his palms toward the ceiling. "What's it to you?"

We reheated and ate the dinner in silence. Brian turned on a sitcom before I finished eating. I could have joined him later, but I had another video message flashing to be opened on my computer. My stomach tensed, but then I saw that it was from wallywonka67, my brother. I clicked the prompt and turned the volume down to not disturb Brian. Wally sent the message from his phone and he bobbed up and down on the screen as he walked.

"Hey, sis! I'm coming over tomorrow afternoon so we can go to that bus memorial thing that just opened up. I heard some weird shit about that place. You ever been there?"

"No," I said, "What kind of weird shit are we talking?"

"They put secret stuff inside, little details that they let people find, like Easter eggs."

"Hmm."

"Yeah, I'll see you tomorrow. I gotta go."

"Ok. Bye."

The next day, I shouldered my messenger bag and swept my dark hair into a ponytail. I walked downtown to where I knew a terrorist had blown up a bus full of passengers two years ago. Some soldier who had gotten wounded in the war took out his anger on a bus full of strangers. The news said he had PTSD and was disoriented, but I think he knew exactly what he was doing. The city erected the memorial last spring on the sidewalk next to where it had happened. They knocked out the front of a bakery to make room.

Wally stood waiting on the sidewalk. He hugged me, which was something he'd recently been doing. He was afraid to die.

"Hi. Let's go inside," I said.

"Right this way, miss," he said with the pompous demeanor of a butler. "Let me escort you."

I threaded my arm into his and giggled uncontrollably until he ended the charade at the entrance. I secretly wished we would never stop acting and that we would walk around the city pretending that it was all our stage, making music with our mouths and marching our own private parade. But that bird disappeared into the distance.

The memorial was a bronze replica of the city bus that was attacked, the Bus 105 Incident. It was meant to be a walk-in museum.

We stepped onto the bus and observed the bronze passengers with their frozen expressions, their meaningless eyes and lifeless lips. It was eerie the way they were posed. Some gazed out the window or straight ahead. Others texted on their phones or talked to one another. But all of them had been modeled after pictures of the actual victims. In essence, we were seeing a snapshot, the living dead.

"What's the weird stuff you were talking about?" I asked.

Wally touched a woman's bronze face. "Look here." He pointed to a man's leather attaché. "This is a real briefcase. Apparently this guy was a writer and rumor has it that there's an actual manuscript inside."

I peered over the figure. He was a balding man in his forties with the leather case in his lap. I unzipped it and looked inside. There, a two-inch stack of loose papers. I pulled it out.

The title page read: *A Time of Renewal* by Hubert Dobbs. When I thumbed through the pages, they were blank. It was just a prop.

I stuffed the papers in my messenger bag as I said, "Come on, Wally. Let's get out of here."

We walked down the street to get some sandwiches. I paid with one of my credit cards. It took four tries before one of them would work. Wally frowned at me, but he didn't say anything.

"I was thinking I would get my own place before I have to leave," he said through a mouthful of turkey-on-wheat.

I desperately chewed faster, trying to swallow so I could reply without a long silence between us, but he continued.

"I want you to stay with me instead of Brian."

I was trying to swallow a wad of bread and I choked. I gulped down some iced tea and finally managed to swallow without killing myself. "Yeah," I said. "Brian is kind of a douche."

"Kind of? Sarah, he treats you like crap and you put up with it so you don't have to live with Mom and Dad. I get it. I'm moving out, too. But you can stay with me instead of him, at least until I am . . . gone."

I sat there glowing. This was my way out of a life that I hated, one where I was autonomous. But it would be bought with the price of my brother going to war. Possibly to die. I wondered if this was his farewell. Heat bubbled in my neck and I thought that maybe I would pass out or scream. But I sat there, chewing and staring at my plate. To an observer, I was unremarkable.

"Ok," I said.

I made plans in my head. I was going to stop stealing. I was going to get a job, and I was going to grow up.

We walked home slowly, arm-in-arm, the way brothers used to escort sisters a hundred years ago.

But Wally decided not to spend all of his savings, so he continued living with our parents. I broke up with Brian and moved back in with Mom and Dad, too. Wally and I stopped spending time together. He grew more pensive and angry as his departure date grew closer; so did I.

~

Twenty years, I thought, as I drove back to my little house outside the city, was enough time. It was enough to get over the fact that my brother was another wounded soldier. He was just another PTSD case, another drug user after the war, another G.I. with survivor's guilt.

Twenty years should be enough time to forget something that happened, to forget the things you thought and the things you saw. I had waited for Wally to be my brother again, to feel where I was coming from and where I was going. But after twenty years, the things we build still stand. Bronze is still bronze.

When I got home I looked at the manuscript I'd hidden away for all these years. It was blank from cover to cover, just the title *A Time of Renewal*. I know now that it is blank not because it is a prop, but because there is no renewal. There is no recovery. There was only a title that should have felt familiar.

"Brother," I whispered, sitting on the closet floor. "Brother. Brother. Brother . . ."

The word broke apart and floated in the air like dust.

◊ ~♦~ ◊

◊ ~◆~ ◊

War slays the brave, but spares the cowards.

- Anacreon

The world is a war; the victor in it is the man who lives at the expense of others.

- Voltaire

Sweets with sweets war not, joy delights in joy.

- Shakespeare

◊ ~◆~ ◊

Neither Sweet nor Sour

Patty Somlo

Al Sharp thought he was dreaming. He knew Colonel Vaughn never spoke.

"What you say, Colonel Vaughn?" asked Al, a nurse on the 7:00-3:00 shift who was working overtime.

"Family," the Colonel said again.

Al made an effort to calm himself, before tiptoeing to the window, a tactic he'd learned after startling several vets prepared for an ambush from behind.

"What about family?" Al asked, then eased closer to Colonel Vaughn.

Colonel Vaughn raised his right hand from where it had been pressing against his thigh. Even at the age of seventy-five, Colonel Vaughn possessed the squared shoulders and straight back of a squadron commander. Al, who had done his twenty years in the Army, waited for the Colonel to bring the hand up to his forehead, and send it stiffly into the air like a determined bird. The old guys sometimes fell into this stuff, and Al played along – saluting and shouting, "Good morning, sir," his stance frozen until the old soldier gave the command for the former gunnery sergeant to be at ease.

Instead of lifting his right hand to his forehead, Colonel Vaughn pressed his first two fingers against the glass. Al watched, as if the fingers might tell him something the unexpected appearance of Colonel Vaughn's speech hadn't betrayed.

"You see anyone out there, sir?" Al whispered.

"My daughter," the Colonel answered, to Al's surprise.

The old man shuffled quietly across the room and into the hall. Al followed him down the narrow fluorescent-lit walkway lined with pale green walls and out to the front porch.

A narrow, winding road led up to the hospital from the highway. On either side, the gently rolling hills were blanketed with gnarled and twisted grapevines. The claret-colored grape leaves glowed from behind. In another hour, the area would be drenched golden, reminding the doctors of Tuscany. When Al transferred here from the city, he thought it a strange place to locate a hospital for treating men damaged from war – a valley that drew tourists to savor gourmet food and taste wine. But by Al's second year, he changed his mind, after seeing the men take quiet pleasure in the light falling across the vineyards, as the seasons changed and the grapes eased their way toward ripening.

Al watched the road for signs. After several minutes, he edged closer to the Colonel.

"You waiting for your daughter, sir?"

The question was met with a stubborn silence.

"You might want to take a seat, sir," Al said, and then took Colonel Vaughn's arm and led him to a rocker on the porch's far side.

"Traffic gets bad this time of day. You don't know when she might show up."

Al, of course, had other patients to look after and needed to pass on the news that Colonel Vaughn had broken a three-decade-long silence.

"I'm gonna go inside, sir. I'll check and see if we've heard anything."

As soon as Al left, Colonel Vaughn pulled the letter from

his pocket.

It has been a long time, the letter began. He tried to remember her voice, but was only able to conjure up the sound of his own.

~

Lieutenant Colonel Charles Vaughn, Charlie to family and friends, was known as a blunt man. Not surprisingly, he dropped the news like a bomb.

"I'm going to Vietnam," he announced to his wife, Mary.

In a few minutes, Mary would have a plate of roast beef, mashed potatoes and boiled frozen peas on the dining room table, along with a fresh drink. Charlie had just eased down into his favorite olive green chair. The television was on. Neither Charlie nor his wife got up to turn down the sound.

"I'll be assigned to Tan Son Nhut Air Base in Saigon."

Charlie shot his gaze back at the screen. In the darkened living room, the television had become the only bright spot. Walter Cronkite was reading the day's news off the teleprompter.

"Well," Mary uttered. "That's a surprise."

Charlie took a long, slow swallow of Scotch, splashed with ginger ale to sweeten the bite. The alcohol burned his throat but warmed, as the liquid settled down into his belly. He picked the glass up and twisted his wrist, making the ice cubes swirl and click.

"I don't suppose I have any say-so in this," Mary added.

Charlie took another sip.

"I've gotten my assignment."

~

Al was late making his rounds but he needed to pass the news on to one of the physicians. He felt an unsettling mix of melancholy and joy. Like the Colonel and many of these old guys, he'd lost his family to the trials of military life – the unrelenting moves and deployments abroad. He had a temper too, and there had been bouts with drinking that he'd finally given up. The hospital staff and a few old Army buddies were all he had for family now.

"Anything wrong, Al?"

"Oh. Dr. Ashford. I was coming to see you."

"What about?"

Al stepped close to the doctor and lowered his voice.

"It's Colonel Vaughn, sir."

"What about him?"

"You won't believe it, sir, but he talked."

The doctor, who was admired by the female staff for his penetrating pale blue eyes, studied Al's face, as if the black nurse were one of his patients. He would have judged Al to be in his early fifties, with streaks of gray beginning to peak out of his close-cropped hair. Al was built like basketball players had been in the days when the doctor was a boy, before athletes bulked their bodies up with steroids. Tall, almost gangly, but still strong.

"Are you sure?" the doctor said.

"Yes, sir," Al said, beginning to talk fast now. "I wasn't at first, so I asked him, 'What'd you say?' And he said, 'Family.' Heard it with my own ears."

The doctor slipped his index and second fingers like tweezers into the right breast pocket of his lab coat. He didn't have the Colonel's chart and wasn't intending to write anything down with the dark blue pen he pulled out.

"Family," the doctor said, poking the pen into the air. "Was that all?"

"No, sir. I asked if he was waiting for someone, and he said, 'My daughter.'"

The doctor had read of such cases but hadn't witnessed any firsthand. He tried to tamp down the excitement he felt. So much was still unknown about the brain's responses to trauma and war.

"I'd better go see for myself," the doctor said.

~

By the third reading, Colonel Vaughn understood that the letter was from his daughter, Marianne. She mentioned a grandson named Justin that Colonel Vaughn never knew he had. After getting a divorce, Marianne wrote, she had raised the boy on her own. That is, until an overdose of heroin killed him.

The Colonel didn't know what to make of this. The last time he'd seen his daughter she was in college. They'd sat across from one another at a seafood restaurant, next to a window overlooking the water. He asked about school but had trouble concentrating on her answer. He gave up completely when the food arrived, and ate his fish in silence.

He couldn't remember how long ago that dinner with his daughter had been. Neither could he recall how much time had gone by since he arrived at the VA hospital. Some days, it seemed he had been here his whole life.

Mostly, he liked sitting on the porch. There, the terrible ringing noise and voices that kept him awake nights grew quiet. He especially liked this time of year, when late in the afternoons, the landscape caught fire and he inhaled the sweet vinegar aroma of wine.

Dr. Ashford stepped outside, just as the sun dropped behind the hills bordering the back of the hospital. All around, the sky was brushed with rose. Even the grape leaves were drenched with mauve. Dr. Ashford was suddenly transported back to Tuscany, where he and his third wife had honeymooned.

Five years had passed since that trip, Dr. Ashford now realized. He couldn't recall the last time he and his wife Sherry had sat outside in the evening, sipping wine.

The doctor shook his head to bring himself back to the present. The Colonel rocked, gazing east, where the road meandered from the highway.

"Nice evening, Colonel Vaughn," Dr. Ashford said, while he looked down. He waited, but the Colonel failed to look up. The doctor listened to his breath in the silence.

"I was thinking how much this reminded me of Tuscany," the doctor went on. "Have you been there?"

The Colonel kept staring at the road.

"Colonel Vaughn," the doctor said, leaning down. "Al just told me that you spoke."

Dr. Ashford waited and watched Colonel Vaughn. As always, the old squadron commander sat stiff and stoic.

The two men remained like that for a while. Occasionally, Dr. Ashford would mutter how lovely the valley was in autumn.

The doctor ran a hand through his sun-bleached, sandy brown hair, unable to let go of the sour disappointment that a breakthrough with one of his long-term patients hadn't occurred. After a time, though, as he breathed in the air that smelled of wine – a rich, fruity Cabernet, he thought – he was no longer able to cling to his wounded sense of pride. Though he had another hour left to work, Dr. Ashford let himself drift into the lighthearted mood he experienced on vacations abroad.

By now, Colonel Vaughn had forgotten why he'd come out to the front porch. The road was lit like a river of molten gold. He forgot the letter from his daughter, resting quietly in his pocket. He even forgot the paragraph he had read again and again. *Mom is gone. She died of breast cancer on Monday night. I thought you might like to know.*

~

After making his rounds, Al went into the office. The staff had cleared out, so Al had the place to himself.

Colonel Vaughn's file took up two entire drawers. Al pulled a tan folder out and flipped open the cover.

"Next of kin," Al read, at the top of the first sheet, on the left-hand side.

"Marianne Vaughn."

After that he saw, "Estranged daughter."

He ran his eyes over to the box for marital status.

"Divorced," it said.

He closed the folder, not wanting to read more. He hated to think that Colonel Vaughn had miraculously emerged from a thirty-year fog only to find himself alone.

~

The sky had darkened and the valley was brushed in pastel rose. Al turned to his right as he stepped outside and saw the dark silhouettes of Dr. Ashford and Colonel Vaughn.

Beyond them, the valley looked like the watercolor paintings sold in town, to tourists who came to taste wine. Al wasn't sure if Colonel Vaughn and Dr. Ashford understood. No one's daughter would be driving up that road tonight.

Al tiptoed to the railing and took his place at the doctor's left side. Colonel Vaughn was sitting to the right.

At that moment, the last shred of blue was swallowed up in the sky. An orange afterglow hovered along the horizon.

Each of the men soothed a separate yearning. The grapes leaked their perfume into the air. The aroma was neither sweet nor sour, but instead suggested a decidedly complex blend.

◊ ~♦~ ◊

Wisdom is better than weapons of war; but one sinner destroys much good.

- Ecclesiastes

It is difficult for a man, who has war in his heart, to wear a look of peace upon his brow.

- Metastasio

◊ ~♦~ ◊

The Tiger Cage

Thom Brucie

Lieutenant Joseph Tompsen's attempt to discover spies in Mama San Anh Dao's whore house ended in a manner opposite to the desires of his superiors. When he returned to headquarters he detailed his report to Colonel Usage and Captain Loo. He concluded by saying that he felt Mama San was simply an old woman trying to get by; his superiors remained obviously unimpressed.

"All right," said Colonel Usage. He rose and closed his briefcase. The two junior officers stood. Before he left, he said, "Captain, see if you can educate this young officer before we send him back out."

"Yes, sir."

They all saluted, and Colonel Usage left.

Captain Loo moved behind the desk and sat down. Tompsen sat in the chair next to the desk, like a student in a teacher's office.

Ben Loo closed the folder and snapped the clasp with efficient dexterity. He rested the heavy prosthesis attached to his left forearm on the folder and nudged it forward about four inches, not for position, but more to pause while he thought.

Tompsen closed his folder, sat up straight and waited.

"This is my second tour," Ben Loo began in English almost without accent and as crisp as his starched fatigues. "The first time, I was captured. The Korean marines of the White Horse Division are the bravest soldiers in the world. Eventually, my men rescued me. I will not bore you with the details. But perhaps you will know your enemy better when you learn my story. You can trust none of them, Tompsen. None."

He glanced at Tompsen, a brief contact, revealing his intense eyes; Tompsen found his eyes as hard as his body.

"We were on patrol. I was only a lieutenant then. We were ambushed. All my men were killed. I lost consciousness.

"I awoke in a cage. They called it a tiger cage. It was below ground, the floor dirt, the sides lined with tied bamboo. The top was bamboo also, with the poles spaced several inches apart, like a grid.

"I did not know the time by way of a clock, but I knew the moment in my mind, for each morning thereafter I continued to rise at the same instant. There was a brief shadow as the sun began to ascend. It was not yet sunrise, but merely pre-dawn. As I blinked my eyes, the crisscrossed pattern of the cage top became clear.

"I wore loose clothes, a shirt and pants. Nothing else. I heard a noise, and the cover lifted. Then, a ladder of bamboo was placed at the side.

"'Get out.'

"I knew the torture would begin, but I was strong.

"Two guards with black pistols and bamboo clubs shoved me to a hut. They rushed me quickly with jabs and gestures, and I did not observe much, preferring instead to strengthen my mind for the torture.

"They strapped my arms and legs to a chair. In front of me, a man sat behind a small table. The table was bare except for a piece of paper directly in front of the man in the chair and a machete placed parallel to the edge of the table nearest me."

Ben Loo moved his head around the room, searching,

studying.

Tompsen moved uneasily in the chair. "Sir," he said, "it is not necessary to tell me this if you feel uncomfortable."

Ben Loo ignored Tompsen.

"It was not too different from the positions we occupy now, Tompsen," he said. "Only if your chair were in front of the desk, at the center."

Ben Loo looked about seven feet beyond the edge of the metal desk to a spot thirty-four inches above the floor. Then he blinked his eyes and continued.

"I made eye contact with him sitting at the table.

"'You'll never break me,' I said to him.

"Immediately, the two guards slashed my face with the hard ends of the short bamboo clubs.

"It was a good first round, and I managed to remain conscious. Small trickles of blood drained from my nostrils and from one side of my mouth. The blood tasted queerly of salt and the marrow of beef which has been burned by fire, but I felt like I had won this first contest.

"Again I looked into the eyes of the man behind the table. He stood and carried the piece of paper. He stopped in front of me.

"'I am Sergeant Suygen. There are three rules here.'

"He held the paper before my eyes. On it were printed the three rules:

    1. no reading

    2. no writing

    3. no talking

"'Read them,' he commanded.

"'No read . . .' I began to read the first rule, but the two guards again beat my shoulders and arms, while Sergeant

Suygen screamed at me, 'You must obey the rules. You must obey the rules.'

"Again, he held the paper in front of my eyes.

1. no reading
2. no writing
3. no talking

"'Read,' he ordered.

"As my eyes focused on the printing, I was again beaten. This time all of my body, arms, head, legs, face, back, groin, right hand. All exposed areas except my left hand.

"'You must obey the rules,' Sergeant Suygen shouted.

"This beating was sufficient to cause me pain, but I refused to cry out. With extreme effort, I held my head erect and again looked him in the eye.

"'I will post these rules on the wall, Lieutenant Ben Loo. Yes, we know your name; your Sergeant Fong was happy to tell us before he died. You must memorize them and obey them always. No reading. No writing. No talking.'

"He walked to the wall behind his chair and tacked the rules at approximately my eye level. He turned slowly and pulled a small stick about nine inches long from his sleeve. I know this stick well. It was dark yellow, about one half an inch around. It came from a mango tree. I have looked into the end of it so often, I counted the three rings. Even now I can see the subtle white and gray streak of its side. It is no longer hideous to me, Tompsen, for I survived it, and I am strong."

Ben Loo marveled at his own recollection, while the intense Cam Ranh sun lay against the Quonset hut raising the temperature inside. Tompsen felt his body become slimy and sticky. He watched small droplets of sweat form at Captain

Loo's forehead. Captain Loo wiped his brow with a white handkerchief. It had been ironed but not starched.

"Sergeant Suygen returned to me, and held the brutal stick close to my eyes.

"'Soon you will learn to act as your own judge,' he said. 'But for three hours every day this stick is your master. Now, we begin.'

"He then tapped the back of my left hand. One soft, slight tap.

"I waited to be beaten, but that was his only act.

"'Is that your best torture?' I laughed. 'You are less than a woman. You will never break me.'

"Even as I spoke, the two guards beat my head and my lips.

"'You must obey the rules. You must obey the rules.'

"This final beating left me unconscious, and it was some time before I awoke in the tiger's cage. The cage was designed so that I could neither lie fully stretched out nor stand completely erect. To compensate for this, I exercised in ingenious fashion. I raised my feet to the top of the cage and leaned diagonally in order to do push ups. Also, while lying on my back, I raised my knees and did sit ups. Further, while sitting, I relaxed in the lotus position.

"I kept strong. It is the way I survived.

"The next day, the guards returned. Again, they strapped me in the chair. Sergeant Suygen sat behind the desk, the rules:

    1. no reading

    2. no writing

    3. no talking

hung on the wall behind him. The machete was the only article on the table. Momentarily, I glanced at the long knife, and Sergeant Suygen observed me. He left his chair and walked to face me. Without touching the blade, he indicated it.

"'That is for you,' he said.

"So, I thought, he is trying to terrorize me, but I am too strong to be frightened by death.

"Sergeant Suygen removed the stick from his sleeve. He did not look at me. Instead, he looked at my left hand.

"'How is my hand today?'

"He walked slowly to my side. 'Let us begin,' he said.

"He raised the stick and gently, subtly, dropped it against the back of my hand and pulled it away, like a kitten taps a string.

"That was all. I waited, but nothing else occurred.

"'Ha,' I laughed. 'You are a woman. You will never break me using such tactics.'

"Immediately, the guards beat me with the clubs. Although they concentrated on my head, they left no part of my body un-bruised, except my left hand. And again, I lost consciousness.

"This daily routine lasted one week. The second week differed in this way, I did not speak, so the beatings stopped. This did allow my body to heal. Mercifully, they had no other contact with me, evidently an enforcement of their own rules upon themselves as well as upon me. As a result, I maintained good spirits with myself.

"They did not even disturb my solitude with food. Once each day they used poles to suspend from strings one small basket of rice and one tin of water. But they are inept amateurs, Tompsen, for it took only five days for me to count and determine that they allowed one hundred and ten seconds for me to empty both. This time never varied, and my solution was masterful. I scooped the rice onto the floor and poured the water onto my shirt. This brilliant tactic allowed me to savor the rice and to extend the drink by sucking the water from the cloth. I don't believe the fools ever discovered my brilliance in this matter. There was no chance he would break me.

"At the beginning of the third week the tactics changed.

"Sergeant Suygen sat behind the table. The rules hung on the wall, but I refused to read them. The machete, appearing to shine more, remained at the edge of the table."

Captain Loo stopped talking. His eyes looked at the center of the desk, near its edge. Tompsen twisted his tongue around his teeth seeking moisture to replenish the dryness in his mouth. Unconsciously, he coughed and within the same gesture, he jumped just enough that the chair moved a little away from the desk. He raised his hand to indicate he wished to speak, but because he blinked his eyes before the words began, Captain Loo continued.

"Sergeant Suygen was the only one who spoke to me. The only words he spoke were, 'How is my hand today?' Those five words. The number five, like five fingers.

"Every day the same ritual. The two guards strapped me into the chair. Sergeant Suygen rose and removed the stick from his sleeve.

"'How is my hand today?'

"He asked the question, but he did not look at me. He looked at the hand. One of the guards brought the chair and set it next to the hand. Sergeant Suygen sat. Then he tapped.

"One tap at a time. The little stick, the little yellow mango stick, tapped the hand. Tap. Tap.

"No other word. No other sound. For three hours. Never more than three hours. Never less. Always precisely three hours. Tap. Tap.

"I see by your raised eyebrows, Tompsen, that you want to know how I know this." He raised his voice slightly. "Sergeant Suygen said it was so. It must be so," he insisted. "Do not doubt, Tompsen."

These last words he shouted. Tompsen sat straight in the chair, his spine touched nothing, his eyes as big as mangos.

"Sir," he said, "I wasn't doubting. In fact, I'm sure you are correct. And, I should really get going now."

Captain Loo moved his eyes from the desk to Tompsen's face. He inhaled, and before his chest filled with air, he continued, as if Tompsen had not spoken, almost as if Tompsen were not present.

"I tried tactics. Of course I tried tactics. I thought about calling out. I intended to make elaborate gestures. But Sergeant Suygen merely gestured at the rule sheet on the wall, which I would not read.

"Every day. 'How is my hand today?' Tap. Tap.

"Tap.

"I remained enough in control of myself to continue to exercise. Those many hours alone in the cage I stayed strong. Push ups. Sit ups. Leg stretches. And punches. Five hundred hand punches into the dirt, right hand. Five hundred hand punches into the dirt, left hand.

"It was in the third month that I first noticed an annoyance in the left hand. As I prepared to do push ups, the hand went limp. It dangled at the end of the arm, flopping as a leaf might flop which has turned brown from abuse.

"Immediately, I lifted the thing, and squeezed it. I held it, hugged it, cradled it to my chest.

"The hand began to tingle, and finally, to throb. I spoke to it softly. 'Do not worry, brother hand,' I said. 'Remain strong,' I encouraged it. But it began to agonize. To comfort the hand I sat in the corner with my back against the bamboo. With the hand against my breast and covered with my right hand, I soothed it, and slept in the sitting position.

"The next morning, I was fine, ready for him. They strapped me to the chair. Intentionally, I refused to read the printed rules. Sergeant Suygen sat down in the chair. I felt strong.

"'How is my hand today?'

"At the sound of his voice, a peculiar feeling entered his hand, rather, my hand; a profound feeling, a sense of detachment. As Sergeant Suygen tapped the hand, tap . . . tap . . . tap . . . the hand left me, as a spring bird might abandon the branch of a tree, gently, happily, it floated.

"Naturally, I commanded it to return to my wrist immediately. It obeyed, and at precisely the same instant Sergeant Suygen finished.

"There was no need to push me that day. I walked into the cage as if there were no other reality for us, for the hand and me. The waste pail, always emptied during Sergeant Suygen's three hour attack upon my hand, was empty.

"But behind the bamboo sides, sturdy and oppressive, I knew the ground swelled and would one day collapse upon me; and the sun, ponderous and heavy, filled the space of the overhead cage door; it grew and swelled, malicious and monstrous.

"I had to act. I stooped. I pushed my head against the bars, and I pushed my good hand, my faithful hand, against the wall. I stretched and pushed with more than human greatness for enough of a period of time that the swelling of the ground shrank and the fullness of the sun subsided.

"For the moment I was safe, but I was exhausted, so I slept. My faithful hand created a restful pillow, and the rebellious hand, the traitorous hand, the Sergeant Suygen hand, fell flat and opened on the dirt.

"I awoke later, rested, relieved that I had found such inner strength to control the forces of soil and sun. I remained in the comfortable position on my side, my thighs snug against my stomach and my right arm a pillow for my head. The useless hand, unable to face me, tried to turn its palm to the floor.

"'You no longer deserve to be my hand. I don't wish to see you any longer.'

"Immediately, upon not forming these words, I dismissed this failure of a hand. I sat up, and dug my faithful fingers into the dirt to make a proper grave for the foul smelling hand. I buried it. Then, out of sight, the incorrigible thing could speak no more.

"I sat still. The quiet of the late afternoon became intensely empty. I listened for noise. I stretched my neck and tilted my head to lean my ear toward the grate, making it available as a funnel for any sound, but there was none. There were no voices and no breeze and no animal snorts. There was silence. Only silence.

"In spite of the rules, I wanted to speak. I craved the power and comfort of speech given and received, but Sergeant Suygen's horrid printed rules which I could not read and could not say clanged about in the empty silence of my head as caged falcons, smashing against the inside of my eyes,

screeching, crashing, in horrible painful silence –
1. no reading
2. no writing
3. no talking

"It was during this time of the towering silence that I began to feel a certain uneasiness. It was not fear, I tell you, for I have remained strong to this day. It was a sensation which began like the far off bark of a young dog, a simpering kind of uneasy yelp in an unused corner of my head far away from my eye but close enough to my ear to be audible.

"I thought at first I had imagined it, but soon I heard it again, this time more clearly, more located, as if the tunnel which lead to the darkened corner were becoming visible to me.

"I felt the pressure of the bamboo as I pressed my back against the wall. I pulled my legs in close to my chest and wrapped my faithful arm around them. By now, it was obvious I could no longer trust the left hand, and I stopped communicating with it, as I suspected it might turn traitor and tell Sergeant Suygen my thoughts. I therefore allowed it to remain limp against the earthen floor attached to a wrist, which by its nearness to the hand, became more and more meaningless.

"I pressed my face between my knees to better concentrate, and I was rewarded immediately with a recognizable communication. The sound it made was R-U-R-T-A-R-F-W-L-F. I struggled to identify in this sound a message. However, it remained too distant yet, and I could not distinguish which corridor of my ear to follow in order to locate its position. The sound was definitely throaty with the indication of a growl.

"I intended to command it to speak with more secrecy, for the rules clearly state no reading, no writing, no talking, and its most recent utterance was assuredly louder than the earlier ones. But before I could make contact, an unusual disturbance entered my spine. It was not pain, for as you know, Tompsen, I am insensitive to pain, but it was unearthly physical, and at that moment I wanted nothing except to lie down, fully stretched.

"Oh, yes, this assuredly became my desire, and as the craving for this singular comfort rose in me, the yelp down the corridor, in the corner near my ear, purred. It was a stealthy purr, close to the floor, and tense. But its volume had increased, and because of the rules, the rules on the wall which are written, but which you cannot read, clearly state you cannot write you cannot read you cannot talk and yet the animal in my head was raising its voice. It might spring to life at any moment, I was certain.

"The need was now urgent to explain the seriousness of its noise to it, for I had become convinced that the traitorous hand would tell Sergeant Suygen.

"Suddenly, the skin of my face became taut, as if, do not doubt me, Tompsen, a hand, with fingers like arctic wind, had grabbed my cheek and twisted with force enough to stretch my skull through it. And the corridor in my head expanded to fill my vision. I peered down its unending length, but saw nothing. The thing, however, growled, growled, I say, surely loud enough that the hand would hear, and I silently, wordlessly, shouted for it to muffle its cry.

"While I was thus engaged, the cage opened and the ladder descended. This I interpreted as a foul omen since the secret in my mind and the sensations in my flesh might easily be informed upon by the hand.

"I struggled to curtail the unrest in my body, but my hips cramped, and my jaw knotted and my head thudded.

"They strapped me in the chair. Sergeant Suygen walked to his position. All things were as normal, the rules on the wall, the machete on the table, the stick in his fingers.

"'How is my hand today?'

"His voice gave him away. A certain tenderness escaped. He must have thought me too ignorant to distinguish such subtlety. He is a fool. Did he think he could disguise that tenderness, that subversive intimacy, that suggestion of secrets between lovers?

"He tapped. One gentle, affectionate tap. Another. Tap. Tap. The plunge and thrust of their hideous union now more clear to me than ever. His hand had become attached to me, and it was infecting my wrist, my arm. His plan was to take over my body.

"The caged animal in my head walked. Its enormous, brutal paws thud, thud, as they landed. It wanted to emerge, and my head reeled with the echo of its boldness. It roared, this time with authority and danger.

"Sergeant Suygen tap, tap. The hand must have heard, must be reporting.

"Don't you see, Tompsen? The rules. I look to the rules. I do not read them, only look, in an effort to force their clearness to the beast, but he ignores them.

"He rises on his hind legs, ready to talk. The stick taps, taps the hand.

"I am nearly dizzy with trepidation, when inadvertently my eyes and the beast's eyes see the machete, and our solution is revealed to us. The hand must go.

"Sergeant Suygen has ended. I am unstrapped; but the beast will be released. I no longer wish to prevent its speech. As I stand, I open my mouth, and its scream escapes. The rules are shattered. I must win. Quickly, I sprang to action. I flipped the useless arm so that Sergeant Suygen's demeaning hand landed on the table. I snatched the machete, and before anyone could stop me, (I was as quick as the beast), I struck the blade across my forearm, directly behind the wrist, and severed the poisoned hand."

Ben Loo and Tompsen were both standing, Ben Loo behind the desk, his fingers grasping its edge, Tompsen several feet closer to the door, his hands twisting the manila file into a crinkled paper stick.

Captain Loo breathed with somewhat more regularity, and he spoke again in his controlled tone.

"So, Tompsen, as I have told you, the White Horse are the world's best fighters, and later, I was rescued. By the time they discovered me, the Sergeant Suygen's repulsive hand had become entirely useless. Yet, thanks to the medicine of the American doctors in Okinawa, I have this prosthesis, and I have returned for Sergeant Suygen."

Captain Loo looked around the room. He seemed surprised to see Tompsen at such a distance from the desk.

"Sergeant Ikara," he called, an order which brought his faithful sergeant to pick up his papers.

Before they left, Captain Loo turned to Tompsen.

"Now you know why you cannot trust the Vietnamese, Tompsen. You can trust none of them, for they are all guilty."

~

The two Koreans turned and left the room. Sergeant Ikara held the door open for Captain Loo, and he closed it gently as they left.

Tompsen remained motionless, speechless. His childhood had simply not prepared him for the experiences of adulthood. What, he wondered, was this war really all about?

◊ ~♦~ ◊

To blunder twice is not allowed in war.

- An old saying

◊ ~♦~ ◊

◊ ~◆~ ◊

Beautiful that war and all its deeds of carnage, must in time be utterly lost.

- Whitman

The chance of war is equal, and the slayer oft is slain.

- Homer

◊ ~◆~ ◊

'Abd al Muqeet

Geoffrey A. Landis

On a dusty street he sells water, carefully filling a pink plastic cup, battered but serviceable, with a heavy steel dipper. There are not many customers, these days, not many at all.

Hidden under his stand, a frayed prayer mat is rolled at his feet, next to the yellow plastic jerry-cans filled with warm water.

He watches the trucks and Humvees as they race by, never slowing down, rattling ka*THUNK* ka*THUNK* across the battered concrete. Although his water is pure and clean, the best in the city, the Americans never stop to buy his water. He was a mechanical engineer, once, a man of science; he knows sanitation.

Other water sellers, not he, but less scrupulous water sellers, fill their jugs with water from the river, where ten thousand years ago scribes dug mud to inscribe cuneiform tablets, and filter the river water through cotton shirts. If the Americans asked him, he could tell them which water sellers to avoid, which ones sell true, pure water. He does not expect them to ask.

(If they stopped to ask him, he would say nothing, even though he knows English from University. Talking is dangerous.)

The Americans, bulky in heavy clothing all the colors of dust, are no older than his sons. They are beardless children, and they know nothing. And yet God, or perhaps Satan, has sent them here, thousands of kilometers across oceans he has never seen, here to his streets, to judge his people, and find them wanting.

Sometimes there is gunfire, or the sound of explosions. He no longer bothers to fold his stand and hide when the bombs come. Inshallah, he will say, if it is the will of God, so let it be, but he no longer believes in God, or even Satan.

He no longer believes in anything, but water.

◊ ~◆~ ◊

The brazen throat of war.

- Milton

He that keeps his own makes war.

- An old saying

◊ ~◆~ ◊

The Bombshell

Muhammad Ashfaq

It is sultry, cloudy, and lush green. Fluttering of the early random red flowers heightens the intoxicating effect of fragrance emanating from the poppy fields spread across the valley. Silence is sporadically pierced by the blast sounds of varying intensities in the mountainous region of Tora Bora lying between south of Kabul and north of Durand Line. Haste of deafening sorties betrays launch of the much-touted summer offensive by the US forces in war against the surreptitious enemy.

Gul Khan and Noora Khan are yoked in a fierce tug of war. Their animals take an identical antagonistic stance by scowling at each other. Gul Khan's black hound is strong, stout and pudgy with a tail as stern, stiff, and erect as a bamboo rod. Noora Khan's is a petite brown rabbit-hunter with a crooked tail making a constant question mark.

"You let go of it, otherwise I call my people with guns. Then it doesn't end for generations," Gul Khan says pulling it on his side with full power.

"Oh, you tell this to somebody who is a Pushtun for ten thousand years. Huh! I am wearing bangles, you think?" Noora Khan growls on his opponent pulling it onto his side with an equal intensity.

They take a simultaneous glance on a tiny little Cobra hovering over the far-off hills then expressively look into each other's eyes. The animals growl and glare at each other.

"You let go of it because it landed in my field, has dug deep down, and spoiled my crop quite a bit." Gul Khan puts forward his claim.

"But it killed my sheep – ready for a sell and slaughter." Noora Khan lodges the counter-claim.

"What your sheep was doing in my field?"

"Why don't you fence your damn poppy fields?"

"My poppy fields trouble you a lot. I know," pulling with full force Gul Khan says.

"It is a crime. Sooner or later they will come and burn it down any way." Noora Khan drags it back with equal intensity. Gul Khan stumbles, but gets back to his feet in no time; stakes are too high to lie low.

"You talk of crime. You yourself hide terrorists in your *hujra* every now and then. Don't you?" Gul Khan retorts.

"You call them terrorists. They fight to liberate your motherland from the infidel usurpers. What about people calling you an American spy?" Noora Khan counter-attacks.

"Damn Americans! I say you let go of it." Gul Khan heaves a big jerk.

"You ask me to let go of something which has come by due to freedom fighters you call terrorists. You blame me I hide them in my *hujra*. It is mine then?"

"What a logic! This is American. Look 'Unglish' written all over it. You blame me I am an American spy. It is mine then?"

Suddenly, there is considerable increase in the application of pull-force; both apply extra energies to evict each other. Dogs look daggers, too.

"I see Muslim Khan over there. Let's call him to decide the matter," Gul Khan says looking far on the winding footpath in the hills on the side of the Durand Line.

"I don't want Muslim Khan. I know he will support you," Noora Khan says looking at the footpath in the hills on the side of the Durand Line.

"But he was terrorists' big supporter. Now you don't want him?"

"He turned when the time came. I don't want him in my matter. He is on your side now."

"He is not on my side either. He is on nobody's side. He is on his own side. You can never trust Muslim Khan."

Forces of pull halt; both try to regain breath and recuperate energy without relaxing their grips. They look searching for something in the murky sky. Noora Khan's ears also try to decipher the sound of a mechanical clatter coming from somewhere far. Dogs exchange a whispered bark.

"We can take the matter to Jirga?" Noora Khan floats the counter-proposal.

"I know why you want to take it to Jirga. Because of your dead sheep! I don't want it." Gul Khan shoots down the proposition instantly.

"Why my dead sheep bothers you? It was a big healthy animal ready for slaughter."

"Just look at it. Maybe it is alive and you can still slaughter it."

"No. It is not. I saw it. It is dead."

"Alright. You let go of it; I pay you one thousand Afghanis in lieu of your dead sheep."

"Oh! You think I am stupid? I let go of something worth twenty-five thousand dollars or more for one thousand Afghanis. Forget it."

"Huh. Twenty-five thousand dollars! It is not a penny more than eleven and a half thousand dollars. I can bet."

"Whatever its value, it is not yours. It landed in my field not yours. You let go of it lest a helicopter comes looking for such stuff and takes it away."

Both look to the sky all around gasping but without loosening their grips. Dogs follow their glances.

"If it had landed in my field, there wouldn't be any issue. I don't grow poppy. I fence my fields. I don't let others' sheep enter and graze my fields. I keep things straight. I don't let others meddle in my matters," Noora Khan says in self-righteousness.

"This is duplicity. Your honesty is confined to your fields and others' sheep. When it comes to extortion of their valuables, it is alright," Gul Khan says expanding his nostrils.

The words of aggression transform into force on both ends. They inconsequentially pull for some time. Start of *Azan* in the remote village mosque operates as an automatic brake on pulling and counter-pulling. Grips are not relaxed. Dogs hold.

"It is prayer time." Noora Khan says.

"Then?" Gul Khan replies.

"We need to offer our prayers."

"How?"

"We place it in front at equal distance, and offer them simultaneously."

"I agree. Let's put it down."

"No. But I don't think you are in ablution. I can't offer my prayers with you."

"Why? I am."

"You just farted. Didn't you?"

"This is the problem with you. You even sneak into others' asses."

This proves a catalyst. They exert full power for a while. Then finding it inconsequential stop, but without loosening their grips.

"Let's put Hajji Badshah into it. We both respect him." Gul Khan releases a dove taking advantage of the fast-fleeting respite.

"I respect him, but he is your minion . . ." Noora Khan hits back, thinking, and looking into the sky and the build-up of clouds.

"Isn't he your godfather?"

"Alright, you go get him!"

"Get him here? No way! He is too venerated."

"Then?"

"We take it to him."

"How? It is too heavy."

"You in front – I at the back; on our shoulders!"

"You are big – I am small. Our steps won't match."

"Still! We can't keep pulling and pushing at each other. Lets' give it a try!"

"OK."

They put it on their shoulders with difficulty; Noora Khan in front, Gul Khan at the back. Dogs follow their footsteps.

They carry it hardly a quarter-mile. Noora Khan stops pulling it down from the shoulder to the clutch of his arms, and looks at Gul Khan.

"What?" Gul Khan enquires compulsively taking it into his hug.

"You tried to push me?" Noora Khan replies with a jerk.

A counter-jerk by Gul Khan triggers a fresh round of sheer pull on both sides snapping the agreement.

"I didn't. You backed-out for no reason?" Gul Khan

blames.

"Whatever? You let go of it; it is mine. It killed my sheep." Noora Khan shouts frowning.

"You let go of it. It landed in my field." Gul Khan resonates the ferocity.

"Are you blind? Don't you see? It is in my field *now*. You let go of it." Noora Khan says incisively.

"Oh. You cheat!" Gul Khan visibly perturbed over the trick lets his entire energy into action.

Both knee-deep in the muddy patch take a simultaneous quick look into the blackening sky, gasp and glower at each other, applying brute pull force on both ends as if for a final round.

Suddenly, there is a bang; the matter stands settled. Hounds pounce at each other.

◊ ~♦~ ◊

War is death's feast.

- An old saying

◊ ~♦~ ◊

Cucumbers

Mira Martin-Parker

It was still early in the day and the warm desert sun felt pleasant against the side of his face. As he drove along he struggled to tune in a radio station, but his old truck had only a coat hanger for an antenna, and he could barely catch anything more than crackled voices. He had been driving nonstop since eight in the morning and his bladder was beginning to strain, so he slowed down and pulled off to the side of the road. Once at a stop, he checked quickly behind to make sure no one was coming, and carefully hid himself behind the open door. As he stood there, he examined the large crates of cucumbers he was hauling. April was cucumber season and he would be able to fetch quite an impressive price for his cargo at market. They had been purchased cheap from a friend of his in Jordan, and Jordanian cucumbers were known to be the best; all you had to do was peel them and add a sprinkle of salt. He remembered back when he was a little boy, children were not allowed to bring cucumbers to school during April – the smell of the freshly cut fruit was so overwhelming it was considered cruel and insensitive to the children whose parents could not afford them.

When he finished, he adjusted his trousers, climbed back into his truck, and continued up the empty road. He hadn't been able to fit the entire load in the back, so one of the crates was resting beside him on the passenger seat. They were the thin Persian variety, and several were so small they had escaped from the slats and were now rolling around playfully on the floor. One began making its way dangerously close to his accelerator, so he leaned down, grabbed it, and chucked it out the open window. He watched as it flew through the air and hit the sand. Immediately he felt guilty. So many people were going without any fresh produce at all. These days, even boiled cabbage was a luxury. Why, there wasn't a child on his street that wouldn't sweep several courtyards in exchange for that one skinny little cucumber.

After driving another twenty-five miles he reached a checkpoint. There were three U.S. Military Humvees parked in front and several American soldiers with machine guns standing beside them. About ten feet away, a group of Iraqi soldiers were leaning against an old Land Rover and chatting casually amongst themselves.

He slowed down, and when he was close enough to see their faces, he waved a friendly greeting at the Iraqis. By this time the men were standing at attention, waiting to check him through. They eyed his truck suspiciously as he pulled up, and he began getting nervous, but the first soldier to approach his vehicle immediately smiled upon noticing his goods.

"Oh my, what have we here?" he said, bending over and admiring the bountiful crates. "Fresh cucumbers! What my wife wouldn't give to serve a fresh cucumber salad with dinner tonight."

And so he parted with the crate next to him on the seat, plus two more from the back, and he was not only treated kindly in return, but they didn't even bother making sure it was only cucumbers he was hauling. Instead, they cheerfully waived him through and wished him good luck at market.

When he reached the crossroad, just before the border, he pulled over and got out. He was supposed to be met exactly at eleven, but he was five minutes early. There wasn't a soul in sight, so he lit up a cigarette and stood waiting. The desert had heated up considerably by then, so he went and fetched a plastic tarp from behind his seat and draped it hurriedly over the exposed crates. As he was tying down the corners he looked up and noticed the dusty trail of a car quickly approaching. His heart started beating fast, but he continued on with his task as if it wasn't there. When he looked up again, the car was close enough for him to recognize it as Ali's primer-gray Land Rover. At once he relaxed and stood up.

Ali greeted him warmly then went straight to the back of the truck. After briefly commenting on the beautiful cucumbers, he threw up the tarp, pulled aside the top crates, and exposed three large wooden boxes hidden underneath. Each measured about 3 x 7 feet and was nailed firmly shut. They quickly loaded these into the back of the Rover, without saying a word the entire time. Then Ali pulled a heavy envelope from his breast pocket and handed it over. After receiving two crates of cucumbers, Ali said farewell and left. A minute later Ali's car was out of sight and once again the road was empty.

He held the heavy envelope in his hands for a moment, then opened it. Inside there was a stack of Euros two inches thick and held together with a rubber band. Wrapped around this was a neatly handwritten letter in English. He quickly returned the money to the envelope and slid it behind the front seat. Then he lit another cigarette, leaned against the truck, and read.

My Dearest Wali,
I hope this letter finds you safe and well. I will get straight to

business, as I know this is of utmost concern to you right now.

The 19th Century Tabriz (4x6 and utterly breathtaking) was auctioned last month at Sotheby's for €35,000. The four Gabbehs (two lions, one floral, and one geometric) I took care of myself, working with dealers directly online. The lions both went to a small shop on the Via Marzo in Venice (a Swiss dealer, whom I actually met years ago at a conference in London). Each piece went for €10,000. The geometric and the floral sold for €12,000 a piece. The rose-patterned Isfahan (unspeakably lovely and by far the most precious of the collection) went to Dr. Bracken at the British Museum (who sends his best to you and your family). We had to haggle a bit on this one, but finally settled on €65,000 – I admit it is a bit low, and I probably could have squeezed more out of the old chap, but I knew you would have done the same in my shoes, having been so fond of him yourself. The Malayer camel hair runner and the Halvai Bijar runner both went to a German attorney redecorating his family estate. They sold for €28,000 and €32,000 respectively.

The money has been distributed as follows: Kathleen received a check from me last Tuesday for €100,000. I wired Kevin Hartourian €44,000. €14,000 went to partially cover the yearly maintenance fees on the Lowell Street flat (as you know, I insist on accepting nothing for rent, and Kathleen and Nadia may live there as long as they wish, but Kathleen begged me to at least take something, and I promised her I would). €1200 went to Ali for his services. The remaining €34,000 I have enclosed for you. Please contact me immediately if any of this goes against your wishes and I will do my best to correct the matter.

Astrid and I flew to London last week and saw Kathleen. Nadia looks more and more like you every time we visit (I have included a photo from our trip). She is doing quite well in her studies, and is apparently top of her class in both French and German.

I made a quick stop by Amwell Street. I walked by your old store, which is now a flower shop (something which made me very happy). The mood on the street has changed, though. There is suspicion everywhere, especially with European collectors like myself (old Mr. Alfaki wouldn't even say hello). This soul-crushing mess has ruined everything, but you know quite well how I feel.

Expect to hear from me within a week regarding the next exchange. Ali has kindly offered his assistance going forward (for a rather generous fee).

I hope I have lived up to the trust you have placed in me.

Your friend,
Walter Langen
Sils-Maria

Tucked behind the letter and carefully wrapped in scented tissue (no doubt Astrid's touch), was a photograph of a pretty young girl about eight years of age, sitting at a large mahogany table and smiling cheerfully at the camera. Her hair was curly and deep chestnut brown. And yes, her dark eyes and chiseled features were unmistakably his. He stood looking at the photo for a minute, then tossed his cigarette into the sand.

It was going on noon and if he wanted to sell his cucumbers by three he had to rush. He climbed back into his truck, placed the photo on the dash in front of him, and continued up the empty road.

◊ ~◆~ ◊

War . . . is toil and trouble;
Honour but an empty bubble.

- Dryden

There's but the twinkling of a star
Between a man of peace and war.

- Butler

◊ ~◆~ ◊

Slain Workers Undaunted

Alamgir Hashmi

by risks, friends say,
as our best newspapers print
and emails confide
in well-guarded spaces
we still like to call our own.
They gave eye-care
in remote areas,
crossing a footpass
sixteen thousand feet above
life and a lungful of diseases
long forgotten.
Their local dialect slid off
the rocky trail.
Then they were out of breath,
could hardly see.
How does death rage in the hills,
not know a place too far?
Tell me more about fear
past the tonnes of snow
over their bodies
in Afghanistan.

Rescue

It was one of those calls,
in the middle of the night,
to the number people are told
to save in their cellphones
if they can't learn by heart.

State workers look busy
in their uniforms and wear
a look in accordance
with the occasion.
They have almost cleared

the ground, and one of them
is doing the last bit possible:
swiping the pouring sky
on a rough
table-cloth found in the bin.

A check, red and white
blocks, for an alternate
view, and a later examination
by God knows who
of their earth-moving din.

ALAMGIR HASHMI

Their eyes pretend
I am not there, and that's

all right. So much else is not
there, and has brought
no one to sight: irrelevance.

Tell me how to face
what was a clapboard house,
with children, their ma
in the kitchen making a meal for them,
their father away at his forester's beat.

~

BATTLE RUNES

Camp Office

Prayers were answered
with little rain
but that naughty bird
sent it down
pat on my forehead
if it wasn't for the windshield.
It runs to all sides and hardens
in your face –
lacquer it would not take.
Not that I wanted my pecap to hang
at home, on a brass hook,
whose very shape
cocks a snook
at everything up there.

In any case I need good wipers
before I land in office
and speak with club mates
on the flying bird-part
and a sanctuary for
what's equally endangered.
Go – try as you may
– see for yourself there,

and there, and there.

ALAMGIR HASHMI

Composition in Early Winter

On this frequency
though sound is clear,
sense agitates.

Familiar birds
wear foreign names
and intone their signals

in failing October light.
Leaf by leaf,
the summer signs off.

I can not help it all.
What is to fall now
will fall.

◊ ~◆~ ◊

BATTLE RUNES

◊ ~◆~ ◊

Small in number but full of courage in war.

- Virgil

The flower of sweetest smell is shy and lowly.

- Wordsworth

The stars that have most glory, have no rest.

- S. Daniel

◊ ~◆~ ◊

Gazing at the Stars

Nahid Rachlin

Zeinab put her *chador* on and left her apartment early in the morning. She had a lot to do that day. In the Martyred Alley, where she lived, black flags were hanging above the doorways of several houses, signaling that someone in the household had been killed in the wretched war. The war with Iraq had been going on since the beginning of 1980, and now it was 1986, and it was still raging, destroying cities, killing people. Even though Tehran was not the direct target of Iraq's attack, reminders of it were visible everywhere she turned. When is this destruction going to end? The words went around her head ceaselessly.

At the mouth of the alley a *hejleh* was set up, a bunch of tiny bulbs lit inside its glass case, and an enlarged photograph of a young man pasted on its front. *Gholam Bozorgmeh, 16. Born in Tehran, Martyred on September 1983 in the holy war, fighting the evil Saddam Hussein and his ally, the Great Satan, America*, was written in red ink beneath the photograph. Tears gathered in Zeinab's eyes. Ali, her son, was 16 now and about to be drafted. Would she be able to get him exempted from it?

It had been wonderful last night to lie under the mosquito netting on the roof, looking up at the stars and seeing a trembling light that made her feel God was showing a bit of himself to her. That had excited her so much that she had sat up and stared for a long time, hoping for more signs. The sky was dazzling with all the stars, large and clear . . .

On Ghanat Abad Avenue there was another *hejleh* right next

to the beet stall. The vendor in the stall was shouting, "I have the best, the sweetest beets in Tehran, they taste like sugar." The vendor is so oblivious of the *hejleh*, Zeinab thought indignantly. But then she thought, that is one way to deal with the ever-present tragedy.

She walked rapidly towards the bus station. She bought a ticket and got on the bus going to Ghom. She sat by the window and looked out, but her mind was filled with images of herself going from office to office until she had gotten an appointment with Ayatollah Moghadessi about Ali, and then the meeting they had in a mosque.

"Don't you want your son to give himself up to the holy cause? If he's martyred his soul will go directly to heaven." Ayatollah Moghadessi was a young man, but his long dark beard and somber way of talking made him seem old for his age. "All the sins either one of you might have committed will be forgiven by God. What is the brief, wretched life we lead on this earth, compared to the blissful eternity in heaven?"

"Ayatollah Moghadessi, he's my only son. My husband divorced me, but my son chose to live with me. I have no one else in the world. The only work I can find is some cleaning for rich people, but that's only enough to pay our rent. My son works long hours at a gas station when his last class in high school is over."

"Do you have proof that he's your only son?"

"I can get proof," she stammered. "Before him I gave birth to two other boys, but they both died when they were children." The pain of those losses rushed back.

"Well then, take their death certificates and your divorce document to War-Related-Matters Office," the Ayatollah said, waving his hand, letting her know that she should leave now.

Would she be able to get proof from the man in the morgue? Who knows if he is still there, or if they keep records of all the dead people who pass through the morgue? The cemetery where her sons were buried was demolished by a bomb, their birth certificates lost in a move from where she lived with her husband to her present place.

"I'm running away from my husband," Zeinab heard the woman sitting in the seat in front of her say to another woman. "He's frightening, the way he goes into a rage and starts throwing things at me."

She was so frightened of her husband, Zeinab thought. He had taken her only daughter, Nasrin from her and had forbidden visits. At least her son had come to her. The most joyous times of her life had been when she was pregnant, she thought. The feeling she had then was like looking at the moon last night and being aware of God. Nasrin was a precocious baby; she began to walk and talk early. On hot days Zeinab put her in a plastic pool, and Nasrin splashed around or pushed the ball floating on its surface. Ali was a lively and happy, affectionate, child, smiled easily, and with his eyes followed her around as if he didn't want her out of his sight.

~

Zeinab got off the bus in Ghom and after she had walked a few blocks, she recalled where the mortuary was. She started in its direction. The streets were teeming with cars racing by and pedestrians going in and out of shops.

The mortuary was a grim looking house on a quiet, rather deserted street. She knocked several times on the door and waited. The houses on the street were in a bad state, some of their roofs and windows shattered. She heard footsteps from the inside and an old man appeared at the door.

"Yes," he said. He had yellowish, crooked teeth.

"I have to talk to you about two of my children. I brought them here."

"When was it?"

"It was years ago..."

He was about to shut the door on her. She pleaded, "Please it's very important. I have lost the death certificates... do you keep records..."

"*Khanoom Jaan*, do you know how many thousands of dead people are brought here?"

"Can I come in and talk to you?"

Reluctantly he let her inside. Through an open door she saw coffins lying around. There was a raised pool in the corner with several faucets and next to it a cement platform. They washed the bodies on the platform before wrapping them in cloths and putting them in coffins to be taken away to the cemetery. She began to shudder – she could see so vividly the small bodies of her children being washed on that hard and cold platform.

He led her into a room with few wooden benches in it, and they sat down.

"*Khanoom Jaan*, can you refresh my memory?"

"What can I tell you? Mohsen was five years old. He got malaria. I had my little niece with me when I came here. She got frightened and cried and clung to me. I remember a fly was buzzing around the air. You told my niece that the fly was the soul of her cousin. She was so happy to hear that, she stopped crying. Do you remember?"

He scratched his head, coughed and didn't say anything.

She told him about her other son, Javad, getting killed when an ice cream truck came into the driveway and hit him. She added, "I have one son left to me and now they are going to draft him unless I can prove that I have no other sons who can support me. I'm divorced and my ex-husband doesn't send us any money. I can't even track him down. Will you write a letter that my sons were buried by you? May God pay you back. I can pay you some *toomans*." She fumbled in her purse and found the hundred *tooman* bill which she had received for some housework she had done. She needed it for her next month's rent but she could see him opening up to the idea and so she handed the bill to him.

He went to the table in a corner and sat on a chair behind it. He began to write a letter and in a moment he gave it to her.

"This is to indicate that Mohsen and . . ." He had written down both of her sons names, had dated and signed the letter.

"I can't thank you enough," she said, putting the letter in her purse and getting up.

As she headed towards the bus she felt a weight had been lifted off her chest.

~

In the morning Zeinab decided to go to the War-Related-Matters Office to submit the letter and her divorce documents. Then she waited in the reception area along with other men and women. Everyone looked anxious. From their conversations she gathered that some of the men were there to enlist, and some of the women were there to collect compensation because they had lost a son or husband to the war, and they had no way to support themselves. Zeinab was anxious, aware of hot and cold flashes on her skin. It was clearly going to be hours of waiting. She was just an insignificant figure in the eyes of the law, one among many others like her. The woman sitting next to her said, "I don't know what's happening to my son. I haven't heard from him for weeks and there are no reports on him. I haven't been able to find out anything about him."

A name was called, and the woman jumped to her feet. "That's me," she said and walked to an office.

Finally, hours later, Zeinab was called in. The man sitting behind the desk was short, bald and bearded. His eyes had a cold gleam in them.

"Yes," he said curtly.

Zeinab fumbled in her purse and took out the divorce document and the envelope with the letter the morgue man had written. She handed them to the official. "I had the honor to meet with Ayatollah Moghadessi. He instructed me to bring these documents here."

"Your name?"

"Zeinab Abbasi."

He looked through the document and the letter, while her heart thumped with anxiety.

"We'll send you a letter with our decision," he said, so neutrally that she couldn't assess what he was going to do.

~

Zeinab sat with Ali on the rug she had spread by the pool of the courtyard. She could understand why people always said he looked so much like her. They both had large hazel eyes, high foreheads, curly brown hair. Ali had once told her, "Mother, I'm so glad I don't look like my father." They were similar in other ways too. After returning home from a long day at school and then at the gas station, Ali stayed up late and studied. He wanted to go for a higher education, do something with himself. She wanted that for him too, something she had wished for herself and never fulfilled. Instead she had been forced to quit high school to marry a man arranged for her by her parents.

They sipped on glasses of *sharbat* and she told him about her attempts to get him exempted. One of the women living in the row of rooms opposite the ones she and Ali shared had watered the plants and splashed water on the brick ground to cool it off; the air was fresh and fragment. Gold fish tumbled in the pool.

"What does it all mean, one day and then another passing?" Ali said in his philosophical way of talking.

"Isn't it good enough for the two of us being alive and sitting here together?"

He said something strange. "Free your body, free your soul, die and be born again."

Her mind drifted to her main concern, that the letter from the War-Related-Matters Office hadn't arrived. Maybe it is better not to know, she thought. Have a little more time to hope.

A few of the tenants who shared the courtyard came out and sat on the other side of the pool. "Only beggars benefit from this war, going from one wake to another and getting some food," one of the women said to another.

The other woman said ruefully, "I have a job now, sewing buttons on the soldiers' uniforms."

A muezzin's voice calling people to prayers, *Allah O Akbar*, rose above the conversation. *Gather your courage and fight on, we're near victory.*

"I'm cowardly," Ali said. "I should go and fight."

"Please," Zeinab said.

There was a knock on the door. Ali went to the door and returned with an envelope in his hand. He gave it to his mother. "It's for you from the War-Related-Matters Office."

Her hand shook as she opened it. She could feel Ali's gaze on her, could hear her own heart beat. Among all the words on it she could only see two, "Not exempted." She felt a painful stirring inside her. Was God really a just God? Did he exist or he was an invention? Or else why would he take away beloved sons? It was like she was falling into a large bottomless ravine.

Then she looked at the letter again and among all the words she saw, "Exempted." She had a feeling she was in a dream, drifting through a maze of rooms, coming upon a familiar turn or looking out from behind a lacy curtain at a view, at events whose meaning was not quite clear to her.

◊ ~♦~ ◊

War loves to seek its victims in the young.

- Sophocles

◊ ~♦~ ◊

Grief Echoes

Nancy Riecken

They say that time stands still when the bombs drop and the shells strike and the ping-rata-tata-tat of the guns sprays across the open field or the crowded marketplace or the quiet sanctuary of someone's home. Maybe so. Maybe time stands and watches. Maybe time, unlike you and me, has nothing to lose.

Time watched the woman die, bound to a tree with her breasts sliced off, but for the soldier who found her, every second brought terror that he would be found, too. Just another second could bring to them both a release from the tormenting glare of the jungle's eyes: a quick burial in the underbrush, a stranger attempting closure of a life that should have welcomed another day. Was there time? Did he have the time?

After her release from life's bondage he remained bound to her, ever viewing that form whose spirit had flown, free of war and terror and hunger. Free of her child's clinging hand and warm tears and quiet sobs. Quiet, child, or you may be heard. Where are you, child?

Come to me, for your own sake. Keep your head down. I'm over here.

Time watched the soldier die more slowly, bound to her memory echoing more, and even more. Struggle to forget. Drink it, reefer it, mainline it to release the bond, but grief echoed until the shell struck. Close enough to blow off an arm and a leg. Close enough to kill others, but not close enough to release him. "Medic!" he cried. Even then his body clung to life against his will. His brother found him, carried him, nursed him, and delivered him, but not from the bond of grief. Grief echoes. It reverberates through time, and time has nothing to lose.

"Daddy. I want to be a soldier."

"I'm proud of you, son."

"Keep your head down, soldier. I said down!"

Down, son. Down, daughter. Stay under cover. Listen to me, now.

It was a longer life than he'd imagined he would live. He saw more than he wanted. He saw the end of one war and the beginning of more. With the rest of the world he watched the bombs drop on Kuwait City. He saw the reporter on the rooftop, and he heard the soldiers cry out.

He heard the excuses for war, and the justifications for putting men and women in front of and behind the guns and the tanks and the missiles. He watched people nod their heads and raise their fists and cry out and agree to make war. Yes, they would sacrifice themselves, if need be, for the higher cause and the greater good. Peace on earth. Good will to men.

He watched real war, and his grief joined and echoed with those who returned in part, not whole. They came home, or where home used to be. They returned to families or to empty places, seeking rest. He waited with them for release. Time watched and waited.

He watched war made with strict intention. Deliberate starvation or torment or terror. Broadcast executions. Justification in the name some greater good. Time waited patiently for that greater good to show itself. After all, it had nothing to lose.

He watched make-believe war as well. It was ever-present. It could be re-wound and played again and again. Deleted scenes could be resurrected. Special effects made it all so much better. And honestly, no one could tell the difference. Except the ones released from the echoing grief.

Grief echoed through the caverns of the city so nice they named it twice, newly punctured and covered in ashes. Grief echoed through the parking garages filled with cars whose owners never returned. Grief echoed through the villages strafed by soldiers who never saw the faces. Grief echoed through the flaming descent of planes filled with tourists whose vacations were cut short for the greater good.

Bury the bodies. Mark the graves. Perform the oblations. Grieve your losses, if you have time.

Peace. Peace. There is no peace. Grief echoes.

There is the matter of containment. He'd learned about that. Good memories picked up from the ground zeros of his life. A fenced pasture of sweet-smelling clover and sociable, contented cobs. A village full of close-knit families. Hands stretched out in welcome, meals shared, a spontaneous game of catch. A new school for shy, excited young girls who hungered to discover meaning in the mysterious symbols. Someone's wedding day. There is a joyful containment here. It is a precious gift, a memory that lasts a . . . lifetime. Has, in fact, lasted for many lifetimes.

There is containment in a minefield as well. Close, spontaneous, and irreversible. He remembers containment in a peculiar, special chamber, where the light is always on and people come and go and come back again and again. Grief echoes there.

Containment's intent is derided in a place boys learn to kill and hate and make bombs out of found objects, like plastic bottles and nylon stockings and nails. What a sight that is to see! What a work is man! What memories are made here to last a . . . lifetime! Grief echoes.

Containment limits the spill of damage to our plans and strategies. Of course, there will be collateral damage. We discuss it and advise, weighing the options for and against. It all depends on which way the wind blows. We explain the necessity for it for the greater good. After all, we have to expect some losses.

Man is born to trouble as surely as the sparks fly upward. Cries spew out and overflow and pour forth. They go on. And on. And on. The world itself cannot contain the grief that echoes into the highest heaven and the deepest hell.

Listen to me now. Stop this.

"I'm proud of you, son. I love you, but I need to talk to you."

When will pride be willing to just say "no"? Let the echoes of grief die away. Be released.

No! Not this time.

No! Not this time.

No! Not his time.

Not his time.

Not time.

Not time!

Time.

Time.

What more have you got to lose?

◊ ~ ♦ ~ ◊

The Ice Storm

Rebecca Newth

The ice storm had not come yet. It was still two hours away. The big cat came into the room, stopped, stared intensely at something while the small cat sat on a chair. He had lived beside that cat for years, yet his method of entering that way seemed a kind of language. What was he trying to say? He'd never seen trees move so wildly.

"Is he dying?" screamed the little boy, and both cats jumped under the sofa.

"He's dying. Daddy, look at his color." The Clingers kept a chameleon in a glass aquarium. As it got colder, the chameleon had begun to turn from bright green to light brown. The house was heated with electricity. As late afternoon approached, the electricity went out and the Clingers realized the chameleon was going to freeze.

"Hurry up!"

It had been raining and the rain had turned to ice. The walkways were icy, but there was a neighbor just across the road that heated with gas. The chameleon's fingers and toes were black now, and they looked like they might break off, so Mr. Clinger called his neighbor to ask if the chameleon could spend the night. His neighbors were able to accept his call, but they noticed, by looking out the window, that their phone line was lying on the ground pinned by a giant sycamore.

The largest trees were bent down under half an inch of ice. It was these giants that would suffer, as the sycamore had done, the ones people had wrapped their arms around and refused to let chain saws get, the ones that stood on empty lots that people forgot, the great black walnuts and pecans from Confederate times that creaked menacingly out of a weight too vast to maintain, the mulberry with a plaque in brass on its girth that read *Designated Grand Champion: Largest Paper Mulberry in Arkansas.*

~

Jean Rowe put the plaque there last summer and now she was looking out her kitchen window. A squirrel had crept into her wire compost cage and settled into the oak leaves. A few minutes more revealed another smaller one. They were resting together to stay dry and the smaller one began to climb upon her back. That one steadied himself with back legs and feet. Abruptly something gave way; he lost his grip and fell over backwards into the leaves. After several false moves they secured a position together amid the shifting and icing-over leaves and eventually they sank out of sight.

~

When the power had been out for several hours Roan Stephen that afternoon put on a jacket and boots and told his wife he would go check on Jean Rowe. He was surprised when he entered the outside world. How altered it was! The drizzle had turned rapidly to ice. Trees were hunched over and humbled, every twig was coated, each wire overhead, each pole. No light appeared in any house, no vehicle went on the road. Roan noticed Mr. Hall went down the sidewalk in order to take his ancient lab out to relieve himself. Roan went on, slipping occasionally, until he came to Jean Rowe's house. One of her red buds had split and fallen on her beloved bird feeders, smacking them totally to the ground. Roan hazarded the front steps and saw candle light and the back of Jean

Rowe's head as she sat by the fire. He'd decided he'd ask her to come to his house to stay with his wife and son.

Inside the house, Jean Rowe's corgi went to greet him. The corgi did not notice when the electricity went off nor was he bothered by the sleet on the windows. He hated the crashing of trees, but when Roan came to the front door he was wild with happiness for he loved visitors. His mistress was in front of a fireplace and to Roan looking in, it was only a so-so fire. It would not do. Furthermore, her truck and her old car, while not having been hit so far, were covered in ice, and limbs had landed so that she could not get out.

Roan Stephen went inside. The corgi jumped on his pants. Jean Rowe hopped up from the sofa, let newspapers fly, and closed a cell phone. She told Roan that she was not quite ready to leave but that she had made plans for where she would go as soon as she got things together to take with her. She thanked him for his offer to have her stay with his family.

~

Mike Gray was reading a WWII ration book and writing in a bird journal. He couldn't make decisions quickly and he hadn't. He too had hold of a cell phone but he was also looking at a pamphlet as he sat at the kitchen table.

"Rationing is a vital part of your country's war effort," he read. "This book is your Government's guarantee of your fair share of goods made scarce by war, to which the stamps contained herein will be assigned as the need arises."

The booklet was a grey-green color and the grammar and spelling were perfect. Somehow our government officials no longer use or know grammar, he thought. Just yesterday on TV he had heard a commentator say, "Her and her mother want to New York." On a menu recently he read that for dessert a chocolate mouse would be served. It was shocking.

~

"Such action, like treason, helps the enemy," spoke the government bulletin. Here was the word 'enemy' capitalized as the word 'government' had been and here was the word 'treason.' Words like treason and government in capital letters he found quaint. *Be guided by the rule:* the booklet went on: *"If you don't need it, DON'T BUY IT."* The cell phone rang. It was his daughter.

"Dad, what are you going to do?" So her phone line wasn't down.

"About what?"

"About the ice storm."

The application for receiving a copy of War Ration Book No. 3 should be sent to Detroit, Michigan with a 6 cents stamp, he read, turning the booklet over to inspect its back.

"Dad?"

Mike was from Michigan where during the war the auto plants began making bombers but the air raids were just for practice. Mike wanted to write about the life of a man in a Boeing plant, a memoir.

"I'll call you back," he told his daughter and hung up.

~

That night, awakened by the cold and by some slight whisper whisper whisper sound, Eva Kreidel got out of bed. She went to the window to see trees racked with glittering ice. Eva lived alone. She put coffee on and warmed a piece of coffee cake covered with brown sugar. She had not thought she might lose her electricity and her phone service or the tree by her front door. Eva had no gas stove or wood burning fireplace, or even very many candles – so she went back to bed.

The electricity went out and her phone went dead. The clock on the wall that kept her company all night was still, its ticking, like the sound of someone chewing, had gone silent. Now she sat up. In Hamburg during the bombing, she and her mother had gone underground during aid raids and she could remember listening to the sounds overhead while sitting in the dark. They sat on paint cans because there were not seats enough. Everyone listened to the plane engines and explosions overhead and nobody talked. The fear of that time crept back into Eva's heart again as if it had always belonged there.

No matter that she lived now in Arkansas or that fifty years had passed. Eva remembered burying cheese in the backyard and digging it up again in the cold garden. Eva was a little girl who hadn't lived yet holding a frozen cloth in her hands. Eva was sitting in the underground tunnel while the thudding and hissing and explosives never stopped overhead. Just then the tree near the front door cracked, split, and fell with terrible force upon her house pulling out wires and blocking her door.

~

In the morning the sun came out. The Clingers' big cat sat at the window and watched a gray tiger limp across the road. A bird dropped suddenly out of a tree to the snow. The Clingers' cat let out a rattle of desire. After this the chameleon didn't die. It turned a spring green. It ate a strawberry.

◊ ~♦~ ◊

Biographical Notes on Contributors –
Including Previous Publication Acknowledgments

Muhammad Ashfaq is a Pakistani writer whose short stories largely dubbed as "political allegories" are characterized by simplicity, economy of words, and a sly wit. He likes to touch upon everything pertaining to human sapiens, their environment, and the interaction between the two. He is currently visiting the U.S. as a Fulbright Scholar, but lives and works in Islamabad with his wife and two sons.

Thom Brucie has published fiction and poetry in a variety of literary journals and presses. A book of short stories, *Still Waters: Five Stories*, was a nominee for a Georgia Author of the Year Award in the short fiction genre. A poetry chapbook, *Moments Around The Campfire With A Vietnam Vet*, was published by Cervena Barva Press. He teaches creative writing and American Literature at Brewton-Parker College.

John Gifford is a professional writer specializing in travel, and in providing marketing, branding, and public-relations copy to organizations in both the for-profit and not-for-profit sectors. Gifford served with the U.S. Marines in the Persian Gulf War, and later received his MFA in fiction from the University of Central Oklahoma. Visit him on the Web at www.john-gifford.com

Winner of the Illinois Arts Award for Poetry, short-listed for the Bakeless Award, and nominated for two Pushcart Prizes and a Pulitzer, John Guzlowski is the author of three books of poems about his parents' experiences in Nazi concentration camps: *Language of Mules*, *Lightning and Ashes*, and *Third Winter of War: Buchenwald*. His stories and poems also appeared in such national journals as *Ontario Review*, *Chattahoochee Review*, *Atlanta Review*, *Nimrod*, *Crab Orchard Review*, *Marge*, and in the anthology *Blood to Remember: American Poets on the Holocaust*. Garrison Keillor read Guzlowski's poem "What My Father Believed" on his program, *The Writers' Almanac*. "The German" originally appeared in *Ontario Review*, issue 67, Fall/Winter, 2007. "The German" is the first chapter for an unpublished novel called *The Soldier and the Widow*, and the manuscript was short-listed for the Bakeless Award, sponsored by the Bread Loaf Writers' Conference.

Alamgir Hashmi has published eleven books of poetry and several volumes of literary criticism in the United States, Canada, England, Australia, India, Pakistan, etc. He has won a number of national and international awards and honors (such as a Rockefeller Fellowship, The Roberto Celli Memorial Award, and a Pushcart prize nomination), and his work has been translated into several European and Asian languages. For over three decades he has been Professor of English and Comparative Literature at European, American, and Asian universities. "Composition in Early Winter" and "Camp Office" have appeared previously in *Arena*.

Margaret Kingsbury is a creative writing graduate student at Belmont University in Nashville, TN. This is her first published short story. Both her father and sister have served in wars overseas, and she hopes this story honors both those who fight, and those who remain home.

Geoffrey A. Landis is a writer, a poet, and a scientist. He has won the Hugo and Nebula awards for best science fiction, and the Rhysling award for best poem. His poetry chapbook *Iron Angels* came out in 2009 from VanZeno, a small press based in Cleveland (and in which the present piece first appeared). He is also the author of the novel *Mars Crossing* and the story collection *Impact Parameter (and Other Quantum Realities)*. More information can be found at his web page, www.geoffreylandis.com

Mitch Levenberg has published essays and short fiction in such journals as *The Common Review, Fiction, The New Delta Review, Fine Madness, The Saint Ann's Review, Confluence, The Assisi Journal*, and others. His collection of stories, *Principles of Uncertainty and Other Constants* was published in March 2006. He has won two Honorable Mention Awards (2004, 2009) for his essays on his father's experiences in the Philippines during the Second World War. One of these essays, "Butterflies and Lepers," appears in *Pain and Memory* (Editions Bibliotekos 2009). Another essay, "The Plain Brown Envelope," appears in *Common Boundary: Stories of Immigration*

(Editions Bibliotekos 2010). The stories "The Pen" and "The Line" are forthcoming in *The Same Press* magazine. He teaches writing and literature at St. Francis College and lives in Brooklyn with his wife, daughter and four dogs.

Hunter Liguore holds a BA in History and is completing her MFA in Creative Writing from Lesley University. Her work has appeared most recently in *Bellevue Literary Review* (Katie Ireland) and *Sentinel Literary Review* (Red Barn People). Her story "The Shield" won the IFWG Story Quest Contest for 2010. For more visit, theworldinthirtystories.com

Mira Martin-Parker is currently pursuing an MFA in creative writing at San Francisco State University. Her work has appeared in *Diverse Voices Quarterly*, *Literary Bohemian*, *Mythium*, *Ragazine*, *Tattoo Highway*, *Yellow Medicine Review*, and *Zyzzyva*.

Rebecca Newth is a poet and fiction writer. She has just finished a new book (*The Pass-Key*) about time travel and friendship during the Civil War for third and fourth graders. Her favorite subjects for writing are our current predicament, nature, and people. She has been awarded an NEA prize and a Fellowship from the Arkansas Arts Council to work on a novel.

Norah Piehl is a freelance writer, editor, and book reviewer. Her essays and reviews have been published in *Skirt!* and *Brain, Child* magazines, on National Public Radio, and in print anthologies. Norah's short fiction has appeared in *Shaking Like a Mountain*, *Literary Mama*, *The Linnet's Wings*, and *The Legendary*. She grew up in Minnesota and now lives in Somerville, Massachusetts.

Nahid Rachlin's publications include a memoir, *Persian Girls* (Penguin), four novels, *Jumping Over Fire* (City Lights), *Foreigner* (W.W. Norton), *Married to a Stranger* (E.P. Dutton), *The Heart's Desire* (City Lights), and a collection of short stories, *Veils* (City Lights). Her individual short stories have appeared in about fifty magazines, including *The Virginia Quarterly Review*, *Prairie Schooner*, *Redbook*, *Shenandoah*. One of her stories was adopted by Symphony Space, "Selected Shorts" and read on May 2, 2010, by the actress, Freda

Foh Shen, at Getty Center of the Getty Museum, LA, and will be audio-taped for national public radio stations around the country. Her work has been translated into Portuguese, Dutch, Arabic, and Farsi. She has written reviews and essays for *The New York Times*, *Newsday*, *Washington Post* and *Los Angeles Times*. She has held Doubleday-Columbia Fellowship (Columbia) and a Wallace Stegner Fellowship (Stanford). The grants and awards she has received include, the Bennet Cerf Award, PEN Syndicated Fiction Project Award, and a National Endowment for the Arts grant. For more please go to her website www.nahidrachlin.com

C.R. Resetarits' work has appeared in numerous journals including *Kenyon Review*, *Gender Studies*, *Fabula*, *Parameters*, and *Dalhousie Review*. Her most recent work will appear in the Native American writing issue of *The Florida Review*. She recently moved to Lubbock, Texas, after several years in the tiny village of Hursley, Hants, UK and then a few more in Washington, D.C. She is acclimating.

Nancy J. Riecken teaches literature, research, and technical writing at Ivy Tech Community College of Indiana, and is Program Chair in English and Communications at the Gary campus. She chairs the annual student creative writing contest/publication, "Off the Lake," and is general editor of the electronic academic journal, *The Atrium*. Previous publishing credits include two children's books, *Andrew's Own Place* (1993) and *Today is the Day* (1996) (Houghton Mifflin) and a variety of non-academic articles. Most recent credits include "Harmonizing the Writing Process with Music Training Techniques" (The College English Association's *Forum*, 2009) and "LOST in the Academy," a series of six games to be a part of *Let the Games Begin!* (Neal Schuman) scheduled for publication in 2011. Most of her academic writing associates real-world issues with the learning process. The event described at the beginning of the essay included in this anthology is factual; Nancy has held it in memory for over thirty years and now shares it for the first time.

Dawn Sandahl is a Michigan fiction writer and poet. She enjoys writing speculative fiction and poems about nature and memory. She is the fiction editor of the new e-zine Greatest Lakes Review found at www.greatestlakesreview.weebly.com and has edited another literary journal in the past.

Lisa L. Siedlarz is Editor of *Connecticut River Review*. Publications include: *The MacGuffin, Calyx, Rattle, War, Literature & the Arts*, and others. Her work was nominated for the 2009 Best New Poets Anthology. Her chapbook, *I Dream My Brother Plays Baseball*, is from Clemson University Digital Press (2009). Her book, *What We Sign Up For*, is forthcoming from Pecan Grove Press (2011). "I Dream My Brother Plays Baseball" first appeared in *Connecticut Review* 2007, Winner 2007 Leo Connellan Award, and included in chapbook, *I Dream My Brother Plays Baseball*; "Insurgent Injured in Rollover," "Who is She?", "ATF Love," "Camels," and "Don't Paint in Camels," all appear in *I Dream My Brother Plays Baseball*. "Don't Paint in Camels" first appeared in *Louisiana Literature* 2007.

Lisa M. Sita is an adjunct lecturer in history at LaGuardia Community College/CUNY and a career services coordinator at TCI College of Technology. She has worked professionally as a freelance writer of educational materials and has published several books and articles for the school and library market in the areas of anthropology and history.

Patty Somlo's father was a career Air Force officer who commanded an Air Evac squadron in Vietnam. Her essays about military life have appeared in *The Baltimore Sun, The Honolulu Star-Bulletin,* and in *Bombshells: War Stories and Poems by Women on the Homefront*. Her first book, *From Here to There and Other Stories*, was published in November 2010 (Paraguas Books).

Poet, fiction writer, and essayist Marko Vešović, born in Montenegro in 1945, teaches literature at the University of Sarajevo. His book *Polish Cavalry*, whose title is inspired by the story of Polish cavalrymen charging at German tanks in World War II (a metaphor for the defense of Sarajevo), consists of poems and short prose texts about the war in Bosnia, 1992-1995. Poems here from the collection *Polish Cavalry (Poljska konjica)*, translated by Omer Hadžiselimović.

Jenny D. Williams is a writer and book editor whose award-winning fiction and nonfiction stories have appeared in *The Sun Magazine, The*

Best Women's Travel Writing, Raving Dove, Ethical Traveler, Prick of the Spindle, and *Pology*, among others. She received the Ross Feld Award from Brooklyn College for the story "Big Game"; before that, her story "The Fisherman's Wife" was voted the top story published online in 2008 by storySouth's Million Writers Award. In fiction, her travel narrative "The Ringer" won first place in the sports category of the 2008 Solas Awards and was subsequently anthologized. See www.jennydwilliams.com. "Go" previously published as "Abduction/Induction" in *Prick of the Spindle* Volume 2.3, September 2008.

≈≈≈♦≈≈≈

◊ ~♦~ ◊

For what can war but endless war still breed?

- Milton

◊ ~♦~ ◊

◊ ~◆~ ◊

ABOUT EDITIONS BIBLIOTEKOS

Mission and Goals: To produce books of literary merit that address important issues, complex ideas, and enduring themes. We believe in the lasting power of the written word, especially in book form. We believe in contributing to a deeper understanding of what it means to be human (individually and socially) – who we are and what we should do.

For a petit publisher, creating original collections is a time-consuming and tedious process, but well worth the effort in producing texts worth reading and studying for years to come. Was it in our destiny to become publishers? We are students of philosophy, literature, and history; we are scholars, academics, and writers – humanists. We are not business people, but somewhere in our intellectual journey we felt more acutely than usual the joy and pain associated with writing and publishing and then made the decision to shepherd other people's work (their voices) into print.

If you like this book, read (also by Bibliotekos), *Pain and Memory: Reflections on the Strength of the Human Spirit in Suffering* (2009); *Common Boundary: Stories of Immigration* (2010).

www.ebibliotekos.com

Made in the USA
Lexington, KY
22 January 2011